Blue Eagle Feather

Sherry Derr-Wille

Published by
Melange Books, LLC
White Bear Lake, MN 55110
www.melange-books.com

I dedicate this book to Felicia Flys With Owls for the inspiration to not only finish this book but to gift me with my BLUE EAGLE FEATHER earrings.

Chapter One

Jeffrey Cooper graduated from the University of Wisconsin in May. Although he wished his family could be with him, he knew it was impossible. His parents Wayne and Susan Cooper were killed in a car accident when he'd been a small child, leaving his grandparents Tom and Cecilia Red Fox to raise him. Now with his grandmother gone since before his high school graduation, and his grandfather too sick to travel, he accepted his diploma with no one to cheer him on.

Of course, he had paternal grandparents, but he'd never met them. Because of his father's decision to marry a Native American woman, they disowned the couple and never even saw their grandson.

It's their loss, he thought as he waited for his name to be called. *I've worked my butt off for this honor and I won't let anything tarnish it.*

With the ceremony finished and his diploma in hand, he prepared to leave his celebrating classmates. "Jeff," a woman called from behind him.

Not recognizing the voice, he decided she must be calling to someone else. Instead of stopping, he continued toward the door and the beginning of his new life.

He could hear the clicks of a woman's heels on the tile floor and they seemed to be following him.

"Jeffrey Cooper. Please stop."

He turned to see a woman who appeared to be in her mid-forties with a slight resemblance to the pictures he had of his father, hurrying toward him.

"Do I know you?" he asked.

"I doubt it. I'm your father's sister, your Aunt Kelly. I've been trying to find you for several years."

"I haven't been hiding."

"I understand that, but when your father moved to Wisconsin and fell in love with your mother, my parents told me you were all dead. I never believed them. I did my research well and found their obituaries, including the fact they had a son. It wasn't until this afternoon when I attended the graduation that I found you."

"Why did you come to this graduation?" he asked, bewildered by the woman's statement.

"My husband's niece, Jennifer, was in your graduating class. We're her Godparents and wanted to be here for her. It was my husband who saw your name among the graduates. We'd appreciate it if you would join us for dinner tonight."

Jeff pondered her request for a moment. His car was packed with everything from his dorm room and he'd planned to leave immediately for his grandfather's home on the Lac du Flambeau Reservation. "Give me a minute," he said. "I'm expected at home this evening, but I can make a phone call and then give you my answer."

She nodded and stepped aside to give him some privacy for his call.

The phone rang twice before it was answered by his grandfather's companion, Alice Little Wolf. "Alice, it's Jeff."

"Is the ceremony over already?" she asked.

"Yes it is. I was planning to leave this afternoon, but something's come up. Do you think Grandfather would mind if I didn't get home until tomorrow?"

He waited a moment for his grandfather to come on the line. "I had a vision last night. Have you found your father's family?"

Considering he'd spent his entire life with his grandfather, the old man's visions never ceased to astound him. "Yes, Grandfather. My father's sister, Kelly, was at the graduation today. She approached me. They want me to have dinner with them. It will probably be late by the time I'm able to leave Madison and…"

"You don't need to say anything more. I've been praying for them to reach out to you ever since your parents were killed. Embrace your family, for this is just the beginning of the reunions you will be making in your life."

"You never cease to amaze me. As much as I want to be with you, I feel this reunion is important in my life. I'll be there tomorrow and..."

"Enjoy your newfound family, Jeffrey. I will not be going anywhere and I'm sure your aunt will want more time with you than just dinner tonight. I will see you next week and that will be soon enough. I have been blessed with knowing you your entire life, for this weekend give your aunt the same pleasure."

They talked for a few more minutes before breaking the connection. When he hung up his cell phone, he turned back to where his aunt stood. The expression on her face told him she was anxious to hear whether he would be joining them in their celebration this evening.

"I just spoke to my grandfather and explained the situation," Jeff said when he returned to her side. "He knew you found me before I told him. He is pleased with word of our reunion."

"H-How did he know?" she stammered.

"My grandfather is a shaman. He has visions, ones that often predict the future. He said he has been praying to the Great Spirit for years in the hopes I would reunite with my father's family."

"The Great Spirit? Don't you believe in God?"

Her question took him by surprise. Would she, like her parents, hold his Native American heritage against him? "I'm a Christian if that's what you mean. So is my grandfather, but he also holds to the old traditions. It is his belief God and the Great Spirit are one and the same. They both hear and answer prayers. I hold both beliefs in my heart."

Kelly smiled. "You are an amazing young man. We can talk more over dinner."

* * * *

Jeff was pleased to see Kelly's niece, Jennifer was in fact Jenny Grant, a girl he'd dated several times over the past few years. Unfortunately, she'd fallen in love with his roommate, Karl Rivers, and they were planning a wedding for the end of July.

He knew now, even if he hadn't met his family at graduation, he would have at the wedding where he was to be one of the groomsmen.

"Honestly, Jeff, I never knew we were related," Jenny said as Karl drove them to the restaurant her family chose for dinner.

"That's right, Buddy, why were you holding out on us?"

3

"I wasn't holding out on anyone. Until today, I've never even met any of my father's family. I guess twenty-five years ago, when my folks were married, his family didn't take kindly to a squaw man."

"Come on, Jeff, you know that term is outdated. Are you sure it was the family and not your father's doing?"

"No way. I was only a little kid when my folks were killed, but I do remember them talking about how much my father missed his family. Thank goodness, my mother's parents embraced him as one of their own. I know Grandfather reached out to my other grandparents many times only to have his letters returned unopened. They've never wanted anything to do with me, so I'm nervous about this meeting with my aunt."

"You shouldn't be," Jenny said. "Aunt Kelly is one of the greatest people in the world. In fact, she's my favorite aunt. I can hardly wait for you to meet the rest of my family. Uncle Mike is my dad's brother and of course my folks and my siblings are also here."

For a brief moment, Jeff felt like he was going to be a fifth wheel. This was a celebration for Karl and Jenny with their extended family. He was beginning to wish he'd gone with his gut and turned down his aunt's invitation. He could have been on his way home to the only true family he'd ever known by now.

Give them a chance; he heard his grandfather's voice within the confines of his mind. *This meeting was not a random act. God has orchestrated it to give you a chance to reunite with your father's family. Soon they will be the only family you have and will become very important in your life.*

Jeff shook his head. *How does Grandfather do that?* he silently asked. His only answer was his grandfather's soft laughter.

Before he could back out, they pulled up to the restaurant where Jenny assured him the combined families had booked an entire banquet room.

In the sea of strangers filling the banquet room, Jeff was relieved to find Karl's parents. Since they'd been roommates since freshman year, he'd met them every year at Parents' Weekend. They'd even invited him to stay with them when he told them about the job at the reservation in Montana. As a stipulation of his scholarship, he would need to work on a reservation for five years before going into the mainstream education system.

As soon as he recognized them, Karl's mother was at his side hugging him, offering her congratulations on his graduation. "I'm so sorry your grandfather couldn't be with us today. He must be so proud of you."

"He is. I spoke to him about an hour ago and told him of the change in plans and I was going to be joining you for the after graduation dinner. I decided I'd find somewhere to crash tonight and leave for home early tomorrow morning."

"Don't even worry about somewhere to stay tonight. I'm sure Karl won't mind if you bunk with him in his hotel room. He has a double with his brother, but we can easily arrange for rollaway to be brought up."

"Are you trying to hijack our nephew?" Kelly said, coming to greet Jeff.

"I don't want to impose on anyone," Jeff protested. "I'm sure I can find someplace to crash. If nothing else I can sleep in my car."

The horrified expression on Kelly's face told Jeff he should have probably kept his mouth shut.

"None of us will hear of such a thing. No nephew of mine is going to sleep in his car when our place is within driving distance. You'll be staying at our house tonight just like everyone else."

"Everyone else?" Jeff questioned.

"Jenny and Karl along with Karl's parents will be coming back to the house tonight. Everyone wants to get together and finalize the plans for the wedding. I'm sure as soon as I tell my brother, Paul, about you, he'll be over as well. They live quite close to me."

"I thought Karl had a hotel room."

"We haven't told him yet, but we decided to cancel his reservations so we could have some good family time before they move out to start their new jobs," Karl's mother said.

He was sure this was something she'd made up on the spur of the moment. He wondered if she knew about this change of plans before Kelly said something.

Jeff worried about meeting his uncle, but would he have to meet the grandparents who never wanted anything to do with him in the past?

"What about my grandparents?" He knew his voice sounded with apprehension, but he couldn't help it.

"My mother died about five years ago. After her death, my father's mind started to slip. He was diagnosed with Alzheimer's in 2011. It got bad enough we had to have him put in a facility specializing in Alzheimer's care. It's very hard to go there since he usually doesn't know us."

The irony of it brought a mixture of sadness and relief to Jeff's mind. Being so close to his father's family, he felt cheated not to be able to confront his grandfather with the anger he'd harbored for most of his life. On the other hand, he was relieved not to have to face the monster who refused to acknowledge him or even read the letters his maternal grandparents sent at least once a year ever since his parents' deaths.

"It's just as well," he finally managed to say. "I don't know if I would be very sociable. I didn't know about it until I graduated from high school, but my grandparents, my mother's parents, tried to contact them several times but all the letters were returned. My grandmother gave them to me. When I finally got up the nerve to read them, I realized they sent a copy of each of my school pictures, but the envelopes were never opened. Each was marked in the same way," he hesitated for a moment, remembering the note on each envelope. In his mind's eye, he could see the block letters reading RETURN TO SENDER—REFUSED. His voice dropped to almost a whisper as he related the words that were so hurtful to his aunt.

Kelly didn't try to stem the flow of tears cascading down her cheeks. "We didn't know," she said, once she regained her composure. "My parents always said it was my brother who cut all ties with the family. I couldn't believe it. I finally found my brother's obituary and saw your name listed as his son, but I had no idea how to find you. Imagine my surprise to see your name listed on the commencement program. I showed it to my husband and his sister overheard me. She was the one who told me exactly who you were and that you were going to be the best man at Karl and Jenny's wedding. It just seemed too coincidental to be true."

Jeff nodded. "If I'm going to spend the weekend with your family, there will be a lot of time to talk about this. For now, let's celebrate with

Jenny and Karl."

Kelly agreed but insisted they should be celebrating Jeff's accomplishments as well.

* * * *

Dinner was a festive affair. Around the table, there were congratulations for the accomplishments of the graduates. Jeff sat back and listened as Jenny's family speculated on her future as a nurse at the same hospital where Karl would be doing his residency in Helena.

Karl's family was equally proud of Karl and made promises of staying close to the couple so Jenny wouldn't feel so alone so many miles away from her family and friends.

From there the conversation turned to the wedding that would be held in Montana in late July. Jenny would be starting work the first of July, and at the same time Karl would be beginning his residency, so it only made sense for them to be married there. Especially, considering they would be leaving soon to find an apartment to rent close to the hospital.

With the congratulatory dinner finished, David agreed to follow Kelly and Mike to their home in Rockton. As though she didn't believe Jeff would follow, Kelly offered to ride with him.

Even though he was uneasy about having a passenger, especially one who represented the family who didn't want him, he agreed with her suggestion. He knew there would be strained conversation when all he wanted was to make the drive in the solitude that would give him time to think.

"What can you tell me about my brother?" she asked as soon as they pulled onto I90 following her husband's black SUV.

"I can only tell you what I know from the pictures in my grandmother's photo album. I was only seven when my parents were killed. From what my grandmother told me, he was a great father and provider. He came to the reservation where my grandparents lived to teach at the high school. That was where he met my mother. She was also a teacher. He loved her more than life itself. She taught English, he was the history teacher, and the football and basketball coach. Grandmother always told me they were very happy and from the pictures in the album, it was easy to see how much he loved her. Grandfather said he was looking forward to when I was old enough to play sports so he could coach my team."

The words came out, words he hadn't spoken for years. In his mind, his parents as well as his father's side of the family deserted him completely. It had been years since he'd even mentioned them to anyone other than his grandparents.

"How did they die?" Kelly asked after an awkward silence.

"Mom had a friend from school who was living down by Wisconsin Dells. They'd been invited down to spend the weekend and catch up on each other's lives. It was Sunday night and Mom and Dad were on the way home when they were hit by a drunk driver who crossed the center lane and crashed into them head on. Everyone died instantly."

"But you were spared," Kelly said, her statement sounding more like a question.

"Mom said it was a weekend for grownups. I was more than happy to spend the weekend with my grandparents. Grandpa took me fishing and Grandma made all my favorite foods."

Talking about the day that changed his life forever, brought back memories he'd buried for the past sixteen years. He'd been playing with his trucks when he heard his grandparents talking in the kitchen.

Are you ready to become parents again, Cecilia?

What are you talking about?

I'm afraid we will never see our daughter and her husband again. I saw a terrible accident. They have been taken from us. We must prepare to contact our son-in-law's parents about their loss. I only pray they won't want to take Jeff from us.

At the time, he hadn't understood the words. Hours later, it was the State Patrol who came to the door with news of the accident. In the blink of an eye, he knew he would never see his parents again. The conversation between his grandparents earlier in the day now became perfectly clear in its meaning.

The next several days passed in a blur. There was the visitation as well as the funeral the next day. His parents were both teachers at the local high school and it seemed as though everyone on the reservation came out to pay their respects. Among the familiar faces, Jeff searched

8

for the white strangers who could have changed his life completely. After the funeral, he heard someone ask his grandmother if Wayne's parents had come. Her answer, although buried in his memory, now floated to the surface.

Tom called them and they told him their son had been dead to them ever since he went to Wisconsin and married a dirty Indian. They didn't need a service to bury him in their hearts.

Then Jeff won't be going to live with them?

No, thank God. We will raise him, and we will teach him the ways of both cultures.

"Did you hear me, Jeff?"

The voice of his aunt brought him out of the memory from the past and back to the conversation as he drove toward Illinois. "I'm sorry. I was thinking back to the time when my parents were killed. I knew my grandparents had been trying to contact my father's parents. It wasn't until after the funeral that I overheard my grandmother telling someone my father's parents didn't want to come to the funeral because their son was dead as soon as he married a dirty Indian. That was the first time I realized how different we were."

Again Kelly's tears fell. "My father was a hard man and very opinionated. I'm so sorry you had to hear something so hurtful."

"I never let on that I heard it, just as I didn't tell Grandfather I heard him tell Grandmother, the accident had happened long before the State Patrol officer came to the door to tell us about it. These were things I overheard as a child and I knew they weren't meant for my ears."

"How would he have known?'

"I told you earlier, he's a shaman. He has visions of both the good and bad news that is coming. It was his prediction I would become a teacher like my father, but that my destiny lay on a reservation to the west rather than where I was raised."

"I don't understand. What do you mean your destiny is in the west?"

"I was offered a position on a reservation in Montana. It was one of the conditions of my scholarship that I work for five years on an Indian reservation. Since my degree is in teaching, I was certain I would be going home to teach on the reservation where I've grown up. It came as a surprise when I was called to Montana. I went out there over spring break and they did an interview. I knew it was just a formality, but I enjoyed getting to see where I would be living and working once I graduated."

"How close will you be to Jenny and Karl?"

Jeff took a moment to think about the distance between the reservation and the hospital where his friends would be. By Montana standards, seventy-five miles was right next door, but to anyone from the Midwest it seemed like a long way. "It's about a seventy-five mile trip, so we'll be able to visit each other often."

He expected a comment from Kelly, but instead she merely nodded her head. "Oh this is our exit," she said pointing to where the vehicle they'd been following turned off.

Within minutes, they pulled into the driveway of a beautiful two-story home in an upscale subdivision. He noticed another car parked in front of the house and decided some of the other people in their party had arrived there first.

He watched as a man who resembled the pictures of his father stepped out of the house to stand on the porch. As soon as he parked in the driveway, the man hurried to the car.

"I can't believe it. You look just like your father. We thought you died with your parents in that accident."

Jeff was uncomfortable having this strangely familiar man hugging him and crying. Tentatively he returned the hug. "You must be my father's brother, Paul. I'm pleased to meet you."

The man released his hold on Jeff and stepped back. "I rather doubt you really mean what you just said, considering my old man led us to believe you were also killed in the accident that took your parent's lives. I'm sure he's never acknowledged you. Hell, I didn't know you were still alive until Kelly called me from Madison. She kept insisting she thought you were somewhere to be found, but I told her she'd be better off trying to look for your gravestone. What a relief to know you've grown into a young man who would have made your father proud."

Jeff didn't know what to say. Finding this family was a bittersweet blessing. Fate deprived him of his parents, but the love of his father's family being withheld was a calculated plan. All his life he'd been privileged to have the love of his maternal grandparents.

"What do you know of our family?" Paul finally asked.

Jeff took a deep breath. "I loved my father deeply. My grandfather told me what good people my father's family was, but there had been a rift between them before the accident. I didn't realize how hard my grandfather tried to contact your parents until I graduated from high school. At that time, I was going through some papers my grandmother left to be given to me before I left for college. I found all the letters they'd sent that were returned. Each contained one of my school pictures. I realized then, my white family really didn't want anything to do with me. It hurt, but not as much as it had when I was younger because I knew I was loved and my life path would be one based on love and goodness, rather than hate and hurtfulness."

Even though he knew the truth would hurt his uncle, he also understood it had to be spoken. All through his life, he'd been told of the necessity of telling the truth in every situation.

* * * *

Throughout the weekend, Jeff met more and more of his family. Kelly, it seemed, called her living aunts and uncles as well as cousins and both her and Paul's children. By Sunday night, he felt as though he'd met more people than he'd ever known on the reservation his grandfather called home.

"How are you doing, Buddy?" Karl asked when they shared a beer Sunday evening.

"I feel as though I've met way too many people this weekend. I just hope they don't give me a test to see if I remember all their names. It's just sad to think I missed out on knowing any of them when I was growing up. I don't know how one man can be so mean spirited."

"Just remember, not everyone is as loving as the grandparents who raised you."

"I heard Aunt Kelly and her brother talking and they've decided they're going to take you to meet your grandfather tomorrow," Jenny said when she joined them.

"Tomorrow? Don't they have to work?"

"Aunt Kelly has her own business, so her time is pretty much her own. As for her brother, I heard him say he made arrangements to take a couple of personal days to get to know you better."

Jeff contemplated the impact his finding his family had on not only him, but also his aunt and uncle and their respective families.

* * * *

Rather than heading north the following morning, Jeff apprehensively accompanied his Uncle Paul and Aunt Kelly to the assisted living center where his paternal grandfather was a resident.

The reception area was very cheery and after they signed in, Kelly led the way to the wing designated for Alzheimer's patients. Jeff could feel his stomach churn when he saw patients in wheelchairs, cradling dolls in their arms or asking where their spouses were over and over again even though the nursing staff told them their spouses had passed away.

They found the older man sitting in the day room enjoying the morning sun. "We've brought you a special visitor, Daddy," Kelly said as she knelt next to her father's chair.

The old man looked up and stared intently at Jeff. "Wayne, I knew you'd come. I asked the nurses to call you and tell you to come here to see me. It's been so long since you've come to see your father." He paused for a moment before continuing. "You must be doing a lot of work outside. You certainly have a good tan."

Jeff swallowed down the gall rising in his throat. "I'm not Wayne. I'm his son, Jeff."

"Why didn't Wayne come?"

Jeff looked first at his aunt and then his uncle. "My father was killed in a car accident sixteen years ago. Don't you remember?"

The old man knotted his brows as if trying to capture a forgotten memory. "Son? Wayne had a son? Why didn't anyone tell me? Did you two know Wayne was dead?"

"Yes Dad," Paul said, taking his father's hand. "Don't you remember? Wayne and his wife, Susan, were killed several years ago."

"You mean that Indian bitch? I told him if he insisted on marrying her I wouldn't have anything to do with them. If they're dead, it serves them right."

Jeff turned and left the room. This was what his grandfather had warned him about. How could a man disown his son because of the woman he married?

"I'm sorry," Kelly said, as she followed him out into the hall. "I thought maybe he would be more receptive to you."

"He was when he thought I was my father. When he realized I was a half-breed, he didn't want anything to do with me. Well, that suits me just fine. I've lived my entire life without him and I can continue to do so. I'll keep in touch with you and Uncle Paul, but I can live the rest of my life without the man who fathered my father. I refuse to call him grandfather, since my true grandfather is the man who raised me and didn't hold the white blood running in my veins against me."

"I got Dad calmed down," Paul said when he joined them. "I told him about you and he wants to see you again."

"I'm sorry, Uncle Paul, but that's something I'm not prepared to do. My true grandfather is very ill. I'm anxious to get back home to spend as much time with him as possible between now and the time I have to leave to start my new job in August."

Although Paul said he understood, Jeff knew he was just giving him lip service. It was evident he thought the reunion between grandfather and grandson would go better than it did.

Chapter Two

As the miles slid by beneath his tires, he became anxious to return home. Although his grandfather sounded well on the phone, Jeff knew it wasn't the case. With the trip to Montana over spring break, he'd only been able to spend a day and a half with the old man. At that time, he knew the cancer ravaging his body was taking its toll. He realized the detour to Illinois this weekend cut his time with his grandfather short.

As he pulled into the driveway, he was relieved to see Alice's car parked in its usual place. If anything had happened in his absence, she certainly wouldn't be there. In her place would be the car of the other shaman who lived on the reservation along with the doctor who'd been caring for his grandfather for years.

"I'm home," he announced once he stepped into the kitchen.

"I'm in the living room," came the reply from his grandfather.

Jeff wondered if it was his imagination that Grandfather's voice sounded stronger than just days earlier on the phone. He entered the living room to see the old man sitting in his favorite recliner and watching some nature documentary on television. It was after noon when Jeff started his trip north. He'd met his aunt and uncle and knew he would keep in touch with them. Grandfather Cooper was another story. He was exactly as his true grandfather portrayed him. Seeing the man for himself made Jeff even more convinced he'd chosen the right path for his life.

"It is good to have you home, Jeff. I trust your trip north was one without incident. To be truthful, I didn't expect you until tomorrow."

Jeff smiled, pleased to have for once surprised his grandfather. After sitting in the chair on the other side of the room, he related the events of the weekend, including the meeting with his paternal grandfather.

"I am sorry to hear the old man has not mellowed with age. Of course, I knew you would find a supportive family in your aunt and uncle."

"Why didn't you try to contact them when my father died?"

"At the time I did not know how to find them. I suggested it, but your grandmother was afraid they would try to take you away from us. I admit I eventually knew where to find them and saw they would love you as much we do. We were selfish and didn't want to share you with even the family who wanted you in their lives."

"I don't blame you, Grandfather. I don't think I would have ever fit into their lives. You've given me a wonderful life that will suit me well when I get to Montana."

They talked for a few more minutes before Alice joined them. Jeff hadn't given her absence much thought until she entered the room.

"I didn't realize you were home, Jeff," she greeted him. "I've been out tending to your grandmother's flower garden. I bet you're starving. I'll go out and start supper. I made some venison stew this morning, so all I have to do is heat it up."

"I hope you're making fry bread to go with it."

Alice winked before leaving the room. The little gesture reminded Jeff of when they dated in high school. At the time, he envisioned what his life would be like if he and Alice got married. Of course, his going away to college opened the door for his best friend, Steve Little Wolf, to win her heart. They were married two years ago and she'd been caring for his grandfather for the last year. Seeing her now, it was evident she wouldn't be working much longer as the baby bump beneath her tee-shirt told him she'd soon be a full time mother.

The thought of eating venison stew and fry bread made Jeff's mouth water. He'd grown up eating the good food his grandmother grew in her garden along with the wild animals Grandfather brought home, either from the hunt or fishing expeditions. The food he'd had at school could, in no way compare to the home cooking he missed so much.

Once the meal was on the table, Alice left to go home to her husband. It was a ritual Jeff was familiar with. Alice put in her eight-hour shift, prepared dinner for his grandfather, and went home for the evening. The dishes would remain on the table until morning and she would take care of them when she finished preparing breakfast.

"It will be nice to have company while I eat my meal."

"I know, Grandfather. I've missed our meals together. We always have the best conversations over our evening meal."

Once they were both seated at the table, the old man bowed his head in prayer. This, too, was something Jeff missed while at school. Even when he stayed with his aunt, there were no prayers of thanksgiving offered for the meal or those who worked hard to prepare it.

"Dear Lord, be you God or the Great Spirit, thank you for all your blessings this day. My grandson has returned to me, Alice has prepared us a meal fit for any king or chief, and you have allowed me to live for yet another day. Keep us safe throughout the night to come. Amen."

Jeff raised his head, a bit perplexed by the words of his grandfather's prayer. "Is there something you aren't telling me?"

"There is much you do not know. I have had many conversations with my greater power. I was assured my life would be spared until you were able to finish your education and return to me. Before you leave for the west, I will begin my walk with the ancestors and be reunited with your parents and my dear Cecilia. This is not said to make you sad. It is a fact of life. You are born, you live your life in the best way you can and then you die. I am an old man and more than ready to leave this cumbersome body behind me."

Jeff swallowed down the lump in his throat. This wasn't the table conversation he craved. Knowing his grandfather would soon walk with the ancestors was one thing, and facing the fact as something that would happen within weeks, if not days, was another.

Throughout the remainder of the meal, the old man outlined everything he wanted done after his death. After supper, he went to his desk and pulled out a file folder filled with papers.

"You will have time to read these before my days on earth are ended. I want you to follow all of the instructions within these to the letter and if you have any questions, please ask me. Now it is time for me to take my rest. I find I sleep much more than I ever used to."

Jeff put off looking at the papers for as long as possible. He did the dishes from supper and put everything away so Alice would have less work to do in the morning. When everything was sparkling clean, he picked up the file and took it into the living room. After pulling the coffee table over in front of one of the chairs, he began to read through the many pages in his grandfather's meticulous handwriting.

My Dear Jeff,

You have been my reason for living over these many years. If you are reading this, I have already gone to walk with the ancestors, or I have found the strength to tell you the time for me to leave you is close.

To be truthful, I long to be reunited with your grandmother as well as your mother and father. This earth is for the young. I remember my grandfather telling me these same words when I was younger than you were. Back then, I could not see past my grief. I did not want my grandfather to leave me. Now, as I come closer to the end of my life, I realize what a selfish young man I was.

You must promise either myself or my spirit that you will allow my spirit to soar without pleas for me to return to you. Do not mourn. Instead, rejoice in the life I've been allowed to lead.

As a young man, I worked with my father and grandfather for the betterment of our people. It was my father who started the company your Uncle David now runs. I ran it for years and provided jobs for many of our people in the process. I am pleased that David now has taken over, and is doing good work for our people.

I've always known it was your destiny to teach and follow in the footsteps of both of your parents. The legacy I leave you is monetary rather than physical property. David knows of my decision and agrees with it.

Read carefully the papers I have left in this folder and I know you will follow my instructions to the letter.

Tears welled up in Jeff's eyes blurring the letters on the paper he held in his hand. How could his grandfather ask him not to mourn?

In desperation, he got up from the chair and went outside. Once Jeff knew he was far enough away from the house that making a call wouldn't disturb his grandfather's rest, he pulled out his cell phone and placed a call to his Uncle David.

"I didn't know you were home yet, Jeff," David greeted him. "Dad said he didn't expect you until tomorrow."

"There was a change of plans. I know it's getting late, but can I come over and talk to you?"

"Late? Is this my college student nephew talking? I thought you college guys partied all night and got along on little or no sleep."

Jeff looked at his watch. It was only seven in the evening and yet it seemed so much later. "I wasn't exactly a party animal while I was at school."

David laughed at his statement. "I'm usually up until midnight. Your Aunt Betty calls me a night owl and says she knows that must be my Spirit Guide. Why don't you come over now?"

Jeff agreed and left a hasty note for his grandfather. He certainly didn't want the old man getting up and wondering why he was alone in the house.

Since David lived close by, Jeff decided not to bother taking his car. Instead, he walked the few blocks separating the two houses.

David was sitting on the porch enjoying a cigarette when Jeff came up the steps.

"Did the old man have the gall to hit you with the 'I'm dying shit' on your first night home?"

"He's serious Uncle David."

"I know he is. I just wish he would have let you get some down time before he dropped it on you. He told me what you went through with meeting your father's family."

"When did he tell you that?"

"Right after you called to say you were going home with your aunt. He said he'd had a vision and knew you'd be disappointed when you went to see your Grandfather Cooper."

"Don't call him that. He doesn't deserve the title. I have to admit it was quite the experience. I actually liked Aunt Kelly and Uncle Paul. It was when they took me to see the old man that I lost it. He called my

18

mother a dirty Indian Bitch. In all the time I was at the University, I never felt embarrassed about my Native American heritage. After meeting that old man, I wanted to take a shower. Instead, I took out my frustrations behind the wheel. It's a wonder I didn't get picked up for speeding."

"Just remember to curb that temper of yours, Jeff. I'm sure that's not what you came over here to talk about."

"No, it's not. You're right, Grandfather told me he is going to be gone before I leave for Montana in August. Then he gave me a folder of papers and…"

"And you don't understand what they mean. Let me try to explain everything to you. About a year ago, Dad asked me to meet him at the lawyer's office. We had a long talk about everything. He wanted to leave all the monetary assets to you and the business to me. I agreed it was best that way. In addition to the company, Dad kept all of the money from your parents' life insurance policy as well as what he got from Social Security in investments for you. By the time the house and all the furnishings are sold, you should be a very wealthy young man."

"You must know that's not what I want. By rights, at least half of everything should belong to you."

"Believe me, Jeff; I received more than half the estate. The business is worth far more than the monetary assets. It made a good living for Mom and Dad and it makes a good living for your Aunt Betty and me. I've been able to use my position with the company to become one of the administrators of the casino as well as one of the elders of our tribe. Between Betty and me, we have more than enough on our plates. In other words, we neither have nor want the responsibility of Dad's money. I've also had power of attorney for several years. With the power of attorney, I've been managing your investments. I give the old man credit, he was one sharp investor."

"But I have a job," Jeff protested. "I certainly won't need the money."

David laughed at his statement. "I know this position sounds good now, but think about it. Sure, you're going to be given a house to live in and there's a salary, but you have to admit it's a lot less than most first year teachers can make. On the other hand, because of your scholarship, you don't have any student loans to repay."

Jeff contemplated his uncle's words. He was right in everything he'd said. What harm would it do for him to keep his investments for something to fall back on in the future? "You've given me a lot to think about. It's been a very long day. I think I'm ready to crash."

"Just remember, no matter what happens we both have to honor Dad's wishes. He doesn't want us to mourn, but to rejoice that he'll be reunited with those he's loved and lost in this life."

Jeff thanked his uncle and walked back to the home where he'd spent the majority of his life. The thought of being a wealthy man was almost overwhelming. He promised himself he would take several hours tomorrow to go over the investments and take stock of his personal finances.

* * * *

Jeff was awakened by Alice arriving at nine the next morning. He was shocked to realize how late he'd slept. It had been his plan to be awake by seven so he would have a couple of hours to go over the papers in the folder from his grandfather.

"Jeff," Alice called from outside his bedroom door.

He hurried to pull on his jeans and a tee-shirt before leaving the room. "I'm sorry Alice, I thought I'd be up before you got here." He no more than said the words when he saw the tears in her eyes.

"It's your grandfather, Jeff, I'm afraid he passed over in his sleep last night. I think he was holding on until you got home."

Chapter Three

"He was so good last night. We had a good talk and..."

"Face it, Jeff, last night was a fluke. I think he perked up yesterday as soon as you walked in the door. He's been very sick for the past two weeks. I honestly didn't think he would last long enough to see you get home. The doctor told me he didn't know why Tom was still alive."

"He wasn't that old, was he?"

"Do you even know how old your grandfather was?"

Jeff thought for a moment. Age was something that was never discussed in the house. "I guess I don't."

"He was going to be eighty on his next birthday. I only know about that because I've seen his medical history. His heart has been weak for several years."

Jeff took a deep breath. He knew there were calls and arrangements he needed to make, but the realization his grandfather's prediction had come true kept him rooted to the spot. When he did find the ability to move, he wandered into his grandfather's bedroom.

Before his eyes, he saw the old man lying under the covers as though he was sleeping. Only the blankets did not rise and fall with each breath. Instead, his skin was cold to the touch. He had no idea how long he stood at the bedside when David entered the room along with the coroner.

"How—how did you know?"

"Alice called me."

Jeff felt shame encompass his entire being. "That—that should have been my responsibility. I should have been the one who made the calls. It wasn't her responsibility. It..." Before he could finish want he wanted to say, David enfolded him in his arms.

"It's all right, Jeff. This is overwhelming for you, it has to be. I've been expecting it for months. Let me take care of the arrangements. Although there aren't many to make, since Dad has been setting things up ever since he got sick. He didn't want the responsibility to rest on either of our shoulders."

Within hours, the funeral director came to the house and took Tom Red Fox away from the home where he'd lived for more years than anyone could remember. Friends and neighbors came to the house with food and other expressions of sympathy. Jeff knew the food would be consumed over the next few days as well as on the day of the funeral, but for now it was completely overwhelming.

* * * *

The morning of the funeral was bright and clear without a hint of rain. He thought at least the clouds would cry as hard as he wanted to over the loss of the man who was not only family, but also a trusted leader for everyone on the reservation.

It came as a complete surprise when he saw, among the mourners, his Aunt Kelly and his Uncle Paul. Someone must have called them, but it hadn't been him.

As the pastor read the words of comfort at the gravesite, Jeff wanted nothing more than to run back to the house and have his grandmother kiss away the hurt as she had when he was a child. Only now, that wouldn't happen. He was an adult and there was no one to give him comfort.

When he refocused his attention on what was going on around him, it came as a surprise to see his father's brother and sister talking with David and Betty. He prayed they wouldn't convey the same message as their father when they first met.

"We are so pleased your uncle called us to tell us of your grandfather's passing," Paul said, as he shook Jeff's hand.

Jeff cast a skeptical glance David's way. "How did you know how to reach them?"

"You have a lot to learn. To begin with I checked out 411.com. Knowing your uncle's first name as well as where he lived it was relatively easy to get a phone number."

"We are so glad he thought to contact us," Kelly added. "From everything we heard today during the service, I wish we had known him in life. He sounds like he was a great man. It's no wonder you are the responsible young man you've grown to be."

The words responsible young man resonated in his mind. If he was so responsible, why did he feel like such a failure? Going to college had been his dream and yet following it had deprived him of the last few months of his grandfather's life. By going to meet his father's family, he'd come home only hours prior to the old man's death.

At David's suggestion, Jeff rode back to the house with Kelly and Paul. "I'm surprised you came all this way for the funeral," he observed.

"You shouldn't be. You're family," Paul replied. "We've missed out on your life for far too long. I am so sorry we listened to Dad and believed his bullshit about Wayne and your mother."

"Paul," Kelly admonished. "You shouldn't talk about Dad like that."

"Why not? You saw how he treated Jeff. I don't care about his prejudices, Jeff is his grandson, and he was so disrespectful. We have to try to make things up to you. You deserve the love of our family just as your mother's people have loved you. After today, I have a new respect for the Native American people in this country."

Jeff felt much better. The angry words of just days earlier were now softened by his uncle's understanding of the life he'd led.

"I wish you weren't going to be moving so far away," Kelly lamented. "Of course, with Jenny and Karl living and working in Montana, we will be visiting out there often. If it's all right with you, we'd like to see you at the same time and get better acquainted."

Accept the love these people are offering to you. They are here today because they love you and want to get to know you. The sound of his grandfather's voice within his mind brought him great peace. *I am with those I love and we are all smiling at this reconciliation. Know we will always be with you in spirit. We all love you and know where the paths of your life will take you. You have ties to the white world, but your heart will be with those you serve in Montana. Use your inheritance wisely. The investments that have been made will see you through the remainder of your life, no matter how far away from this reservation things take you.*

* * * *

The house that now belonged to Jeff was filled with people, and tables groaned with the amount of food brought in by the neighbors and friends of both Jeff, David and the old man who loved them both unconditionally.

"Your grandfather was one of the last great men of our people," the tribal leader said when he shook Jeff's hand. "He will be missed by everyone who ever knew him. I see the same kind of leadership in your uncle, but it grieves me to think of you leaving us."

Jeff smiled. "You were one of the people responsible for getting me the scholarship and you knew the stipulations of it. As much as I wanted to come back here to teach, the need was greater in Montana."

"Those are wise words, Jeffrey. You will make your grandfather proud with your actions."

Others came up to him, each expressing the same sentiments. The support of his friends and neighbors, coupled with that of his new family, bolstered the silent message he'd received from his grandfather earlier in the day. His main mission now became to make everyone who believed in him proud.

* * * *

Paul and Kelly stayed on over the weekend to help Jeff get the house in order and ready to be put on the market. In the process, David also came over, and together they went through Tom and Cecilia's possessions to decide what to keep and what to sell.

"I can't believe the beauty of these artifacts," Kelly said, as she held up one of the beautifully decorated bowls Jeff remembered seeing his grandmother use during the many ceremonies that took place in their home.

"I don't know how you can bear to part with any of these things," Paul observed at the end of the sorting.

"We can't," David replied. "We'll be donating a lot of these pieces to the community museum. It was my father's wish. As for the furniture and the car, we are donating it to the social services office to be given to deserving families."

"What does that leave you, Jeff?"

"There will be the proceeds from the sale of the house and I have an inheritance. It will be more than enough. Everything was decided long before my grandfather became so ill."

"You know we will always be there to help you," Paul said. "We are not without the means to give you financial aid if you need it."

Jeff didn't want to upset the white side of his family, but he also didn't want them to know of the extent of the inheritance left for him by his parents as well as his grandfather. "I'll remember your offer. If there's ever anything I need, I'll be sure to contact you."

Before they left, Kelly insisted they needed to go back to the cemetery and find the graves of Wayne and Susan.

Jeff didn't want to go back to the cemetery, but he couldn't refuse to take them to the gravesite. As they made their way to the plot of land where his parents had been laid to rest, his heart lurched. He'd come there many times over the past sixteen years with his grandparents, but this would be the first time he'd come on his own.

In his mind's eye, he could see his parents as they looked in the picture his grandfather kept on his desk. They would always be the happy young couple in the picture. They would never age just as they hadn't seen him grow from a dependent child to an independent man.

* * * *

It took only a matter of days for the house to be sold and Jeff to arrange to leave for Montana. He knew it was early, but he would do some sightseeing along the way.

"You know you can call me if you need anything," David said once the car was packed. His words mirrored those of his white uncle only weeks earlier. "We have a place you can crash when you come back here to visit."

"I know you do. It might be a while before I come back, but I'll keep your offer in mind. I need to take this time to figure out who I am and what my future holds. I'll keep in contact though and let you know what I'm doing."

Driving away from the reservation was heart wrenching to say the very least. During the four years he'd been at the University, he'd left

25

several times, always knowing his grandfather would be waiting for his return. This time was different. Only Uncle David and Aunt Betty would be waiting for him. He knew they had their own lives to live and like David said, had a lot on their plates.

For the first time in his life, Jeff was completely alone. His decisions about his future were his to make and his to regret if necessary.

Tracing the route he'd traveled so many times before on his way to college, he drove to Madison to hook up with I90. By evening, he was in Albert Lea where he'd made reservations to spend the night. He wanted to be fresh the next morning when he crossed over into South Dakota. Once there, he would be doing the majority of his sightseeing.

* * * *

The next morning he crossed the state line and took the exit to Sioux Falls. After eating lunch, he drove to the legendary falls. Sitting next to them, he enjoyed the litany of the falling water. Behind his closed eyelids, he saw the tribe for whom the falls were named.

In his vision, the men were not the fierce braves who terrorized the white settlers as well as the army in the area. They were family men with wives and children living lives not unlike any typical American family in the modern world.

We are the Sioux of the past. We are the mighty warriors who wandered freely across these plains. These falls were sacred to us. Gather your strength from their essence. You are of the Indians of this new time. You are destined to do great things with your life. Soon your Spirit Guide will show himself to you. Be ready to accept your destiny.

"Amazing, aren't they?" a man said from behind him, breaking his concentration and interrupting the voice from the past resonating in his mind.

Jeff snapped to attention and turned to the man who just spoke to him. "They most certainly are. I was trying to envision them as they were hundreds of years ago before the whites came to this area."

"You're Native American," the man observed.

Jeff took a closer look at the man. Although his hair was closely cropped, it was evident he carried Native American blood.

"I'm from Wisconsin. My grandfather was a great shaman."

26

"I thought as much. Am I mistaken to think you were communicating with the elders when I came up to you?"

"I was. At first it amazed me, but then I realized my grandfather was probably orchestrating this from beyond."

"Are you staying in Sioux Falls tonight?"

Red flags immediately popped into Jeff's head. "I might, I haven't decided yet. Why do you ask?"

"I'm sorry, I should have introduced myself. I'm Norman Hawk. I come down here often to meditate. My father is also a shaman and he wants me to follow in his footsteps. In the meantime, I work as a lawyer for our people. I know my dad would enjoy meeting you. Do I have to ask what you're doing here?"

"I could tell you I'm a tourist, but I've been taught never to tell a lie. My name is Jeff Cooper. I'm on my way to Montana where I have a position as a teacher waiting for me on a reservation. It was a stipulation of the scholarship I received for college. I decided I'd do a little sightseeing on the way. I have a month before I have to be in Montana."

"Good, then spend a few days with us and get in touch with some more of your Native American roots."

Jeff thought over what Norman was suggesting. He'd lived on the reservation for his entire life, but he only knew the history of his own people. By learning more of the tribes west of the Mississippi River, he might have a better insight into the lives of the people he would be serving in Montana.

"I think I'll accept your invitation, but don't you have to okay this with your wife?"

"I suppose that might be a good idea. Of course, she's used to my impromptu invitations. Why don't you meet me here at four? I have to get back to work right now. That will give me time to contact my wife as well as my dad. I'm sure they'll all be excited to meet you. We get many Native Americans here, but very rarely are they the grandson of a shaman. I know Dad will be anxious to talk to you."

Jeff agreed and spent the remainder of the afternoon doing more sightseeing as well as finding a coffee shop with Internet access. After setting up his laptop, he composed an e-mail to his Uncle David telling him of meeting Norman Hawk. He hoped maybe David would know of

Norman or his father, even though it was doubtful.

It amazed him when people he met, assumed because he had Native American blood, he knew every Native American in the country, no matter what tribe they came from. He laughed at himself to think his uncle might know this man he just met.

It didn't take long for David to return his e-mail. *I wasn't sure what route you were taking to get to Montana. Had I known you were going to be going through Sioux Falls, I would have told you to contact Norman. I met him at a pow-wow down in Peoria a few years ago. We've kept in contact ever since. Tell him I said hello. I know you'll enjoy your visit.*

Jeff shook his head after reading David's message. He certainly didn't believe in coincidence, but how else could he explain the connection between his uncle and the stranger who approached him at the falls.

By the time he finished his coffee, it was getting close to the time when he was supposed to go to the falls to meet with Norman.

He was pleased to arrive early so as not to keep the man who would be his host waiting. Around him, several tourists were taking pictures and he wished he was like them. Instead of just snapping pictures, his mind wandered easily to the vision he'd experienced earlier in the day. Perhaps his grandfather had been right, and he'd been given the gift of visions enjoyed by the shaman of the family.

"I hope I didn't keep you waiting too long," Norman said as he approached Jeff.

"Not really. I suppose if I lived here I would get used to this, but to be truthful I could sit here and just watch the water going over the falls all day long."

"I hear you there. I do live here and I never get tired of looking at the falls and wondering where the water comes from and goes too. I usually make it here at least three days a week during my lunch hour. There are times I swear I can see the braves who camped here long before the whites came and took our land away from us."

Jeff marveled at the similarities between Norman's visions and his own. He decided it was best to play things close to the vest with this stranger.

"I did a little research on you," Norman commented as they walked back to the parking lot. "Something about your name nagged at my memory. I contacted my friend, David Red Fox in Wisconsin and he told me he'd just sent you an e-mail saying he knew me. Your grandfather is a bit of a legend even outside his community. My father met him several years ago at a pow-wow right here in South Dakota."

Jeff breathed a bit easier. He'd been concerned about accepting an invitation from a stranger, but he knew from here on in, every person he met would be a stranger until he made them friends. Having this man be someone known to his family put his mind at ease.

It didn't take long for Jeff to follow Norman to a modest home in a relatively new subdivision on the east side of town. There was a small foreign car parked in the driveway and an older PT Cruiser in front of the house. Jeff pulled his car in behind the PT while Norman parked in the driveway.

"Welcome to our humble abode," Norman called, as Jeff got out of his car and started up the driveway. "I see the old man is already here. He was excited when I called him to say I was bringing you home with me."

Jeff looked at the older man standing on the porch. If he'd expected to see an old man with a weathered face like that of his grandfather, he was disappointed. Like Norman, his father wore his hair cut short and was dressed in a pair of jeans with what Jeff would call a cowboy shirt.

"I'm pleased to meet you," the older man said. "I'm Ken Hawk. I remember your grandfather well. I was sorry to hear of his passing. You do resemble him, you know. Are you also a shaman?"

Jeff held out his hand. "I'm afraid there's a little too much white blood running through my veins for me to be considered a shaman. That said, I'm a teacher, like my parents were. Since Grandfather's passing, there was no reason to stay the entire summer in Wisconsin. I figured it was a good time to do some sightseeing. That's what I was doing when I met Norman today."

Ken nodded, but for some reason Jeff thought he read something more in the man's expression.

"What are you fixing for supper tonight, Honey?" Norman asked.

"I thought our visitor might like some puppy stew."

Jeff could feel his stomach begin to churn. He'd heard people talk

29

about puppy stew, but he never thought he'd be eating it for an evening meal.

"It's okay, Jeff," Norman assured him. "We just call it puppy stew. No dogs were harmed in the making of tonight's supper. Hannah makes it with chicken and fresh vegetables. The kids get a kick out of it."

Jeff hoped his sigh of relief wasn't noticeable. He certainly didn't want to hurt the feelings of his hosts.

* * * *

The Hawk family turned out to be the perfect hosts. Ken suggested he would enjoy showing Jeff around the state of South Dakota. When he objected, Ken insisted it would be payment for the many things he'd learned from Tom over the years.

"Call it a repayment of an old debt. You see, when I first met your Grandfather, I was just beginning my journey as a shaman. We were hosting a pow-wow on the Pine Ridge Reservation. That's where I lived at the time. My father was a shaman and he wanted me to be one as well. I kept insisting I wanted to go to college and study to be a teacher. It was Tom who told my dad I could do both and he would help me to get a scholarship."

Jeff couldn't believe what Ken was saying. The words were the same ones as his grandfather used when Jeff wanted to be a teacher. It made him wonder how many other young men had been helped by the man he called Grandfather all his life.

"So if you were a teacher, how did you end up here, in Sioux Falls?"

"I taught at the school on Pine Ridge for several years and then I was offered the position of principal at the school for Sioux students. I've been here ever since. Over the years', Tom and I have been in contact both about my teaching career and what I've done in my position as shaman. Last night I had a vision of a young man, you Jeff, coming to this area. I hope to do for you what your grandfather did for me so many years ago."

Jeff nodded. He had no idea how many lives had been touched by Tom Red Fox. He knew his grandfather was a shaman and a well-respected one at that, but he didn't know the respect went beyond the borders of their reservation. In all his life, he never heard about either of

30

his grandparents going to any of the pow-wows held around the area. His Uncle David, on the other hand, went to at least three or four of the larger ones every year.

Early the next morning, Jeff accompanied Ken as they drove west across the state. This was the route he would be taking on his way to Montana, but driving it with someone who knew the area was an opportunity he couldn't pass up.

Through the morning, they drove toward the Badlands. Along the way, Ken pointed out places of importance to the Sioux nation. By noon they'd put many miles behind them. When Ken pulled off at a wayside, Jeff was glad to be able to get out and stretch his legs.

The heat of midday July hit him like a furnace when he exited the air-conditioned car. "How did people survive without air conditioning?"

Ken chuckled. "You don't miss what you've never had. Our people welcomed the summer months because they were a respite from the bitter cold of winter. This is the time of work for our people. It was when we hunted for the meat to sustain ourselves throughout the long winter months. Our women also gathered the roots and herbs provided by God and the Great Spirit. Rejoice in the changing seasons we are privileged to experience."

Jeff looked at Ken wondering how the same words his grandfather told him repeatedly were coming from this man's mouth. While he made his way to the restroom, Ken unpacked the picnic lunch Hannah made for them before they left the house.

The closer he got to the only building in the rest area, the more overwhelming the smell of the pit toilet sitting in the hot sun became. He was about to enter the small building when it disappeared from his view. In its stead, a bright light filled his line of vision. In the center of the glow, a beautiful eagle appeared.

Chapter Four

The bird was unlike any eagle Jeff could ever remember seeing before. The bird's feathers seemed to be blue in color and glowed as bright as the light had been earlier.

I am your Spirit Guide. I have been sent to show you the path your life is going to take. You are a special mix between white and red. The Great Spirit has plans for you. While you teach the children of the reservation, you will be taught more of the ways of the shaman. You will make your grandfather proud. Even though he walks with the ancestors, he is never further away than your memories and ready to show you the way you are to take. From this day forward, you will be known as Blue Eagle Feather.

The bright glow faded. In its stead, the stench of the outhouse returned along with the building housing it. Jeff felt something in his hand and looked down to see he clutched an eagle feather in his right hand. Rather than any other feather he'd ever seen, this one was grey and in the sunlight looked as if it had a blue tint to it.

"Where did this come from?" he questioned out loud. Forgetting his need to use the restroom, he turned back to where Ken waited for him.

"Are you sure you do not know? I watched as you experienced your vision. I saw the great blue eagle come to you. Even at your advanced age, you have gone on your vision quest. Even though I could not hear the words spoken to you, I am certain you have been given your *man* name."

Jeff forced himself to walk back to the picnic table where Ken waited for him. Just before his legs gave out on him, he dropped down onto the stone bench, embracing it as though it was an overstuffed easy chair in his grandfather's living room.

"You—you saw it?"

Ken nodded. "It was amazing. I have never had the privilege of seeing a young man receive his vision to say nothing of his *man* name. What name did your Spirit Guide give you?"

Jeff hesitated for a moment. He didn't know if he was worthy to speak the words of his new name. "It was Blue Eagle Feather. I know it must have meaning, I just don't know what it is."

"I wish your grandfather was here to explain this to you. I am not worthy to interpret something this powerful. Many years ago, I was privileged to see a white buffalo born on a farm in southern Wisconsin. That was an old prophesy for peace. It was a powerful prophesy but not nearly as powerful as what I witnessed here today."

Jeff could hardly believe the things Ken was saying. How could something like this be happening to someone like him? With his white blood, why had God or the Great Spirit or this so-called Spirit Guide, chose him to bring the message of the Blue Eagle?

"There is a great shaman on the reservation where you will be working. He is a member of the Blackfoot tribe. It is from their history and stories that the prophesy comes. What I can tell you is that you are blessed. The feather you hold in your hand is sacred and should be treated as such."

Jeff contemplated the feather that lay between them on the picnic table. He didn't want to know anything about the meaning of the feather. If he could believe Ken, it was something akin to the birth of the white buffalo.

At the time, he'd been only four, but he remembered his parents leaving him with friends so they could drive to Janesville, Wisconsin to see the calf. When he'd been going through his grandfather's things, he found pictures of the white calf and the many Native Americans who went to the farm in southern Wisconsin to see it. He'd found the pictures in a scrapbook along with several newspaper clippings documenting the miraculous event.

Surely, the magnificent feather that now belonged to him wasn't as important to the Native American community as the birth of the predicted white buffalo.

Trying to put the vision he'd experienced behind him, Jeff picked up a sandwich and chewed on it thoughtfully.

"I wish I could tell you more of what you want to know about the vision you experienced. I know a little of the prophesy, but not enough to give you the spiritual advice you need," Ken finally said.

"Don't worry about it. I'm not sure I want to know anything about it. For now, let's just forget what happened here. I'm anxious to see the Badlands as well as the area around Rapid City. Can't we just forget any of this ever happened?"

Ken's smile told him much more than any words. "We can drop the subject, for now, but eventually you will have to face it. When you get to your final destination, look up Alan Turtle. He will be able to help you understand the significance of the vision you received today."

They finished their lunch and repacked the picnic basket in the trunk of the car. Jeff took the time to place the eagle feather in the zippered compartment of his overnight bag. There, he was certain, it would be safe. In addition, it would be out of sight and out of mind.

* * * *

The grotesque beauty of the Badlands awed Jeff. He could see the ancient Sioux warriors riding through this anomaly of nature and wondering about the meaning of the rock formations.

"Did the ancients live here?" he finally asked.

"Not here. They called this place *Mako Sica*, which translates to the name Badlands in English. At least that was what the French explorers called it when they traveled through this area."

"*Mako Sica*," Jeff repeated the words that were foreign to him but rolled so easily off Ken's tongue.

"You will see that at the south end of the park is the Pine Ridge Reservation. This is where I grew up. The hunting is good down there and before the white men decimated the great herds, the buffalo were plentiful. We are just now getting a new herd established, but unfortunately, they are no longer allowed to roam free as they once did. Now they are farmed like the domesticated cattle of the white men."

The drive through the Badlands brought more and more visions to Jeff, but he kept them to himself. He had no right to be receiving these visions. In no way did he want Ken to put any more significance to them than they deserved.

Once they entered the reservation, the stories of Wounded Knee came crashing back on him. Events like the Ghost Dances and the name of Chief Spotted Elk came to the forefront. In his mind's eye, he saw the events of the book *BURY MY HEART AT WOUNDED KNEE* unfold for him.

In an attempt to stop the visions, he rubbed his fists over his eyes. He silently prayed to whatever deity was sending these visions to him to make them stop.

"You can try," Ken observed, "but there is no way you can rub away the visions from your Spirit Guide. They are preparing you for what lies ahead for you. Destiny is not something from which you can escape. For now you can pretend it doesn't exist, but soon it will all be made clear to you."

Rather than stopping along the way, Ken drove directly to the Wounded Knee Memorial. Getting out of the car, the starkness of the cemetery was so overpowering, Jeff fell to his knees.

Be you Sioux, Cheyenne, Blackfoot, Chippewa or any of the other tribes who populated this great nation, this is a memorial to your past. Learn from what happened here. It was a decline of a mighty people bending to the superiority of the whites. We, who are called Native Americans, are a proud race. Remember everything you see here this day. Soon all will be revealed, including your destiny.

Jeff awoke to Ken wiping his face with a damp cloth. "I thought I'd lost you to the ancestors," Ken said as Jeff sat up.

"I was. This place has special meaning for everyone in the Native American community. I wish I would have gone to one of the pow-wow's with my Uncle David, but Grandfather didn't think it was such a good idea."

"That's a shame. There's a big pow-wow here in South Dakota in August, but of course, you'll be in Montana by then. I wasn't going to mention it, but there is a small pow-wow right here at Pine Ridge this weekend. Would you like to attend it on the way back from Rapid City?"

Jeff thought about it for only a moment before accepting Ken's suggestion. "I'd like to experience it. Maybe..." he allowed the rest of the sentence to die on his lips. He certainly didn't want to put voice to the thoughts running through his mind about the visions and voices he'd been hearing ever since stopping at the wayside and hearing his Spirit Guide give him his 'man' name.

"We'll stop at my brother's house and see about getting you something appropriate to wear this weekend."

After leaving the monument, they drove to the home of Charles Hawk. It was far different from the home where Norman lived in Sioux Falls. Although modern, the furnishings were simple and it was much smaller than even the home where Jeff grew up in Wisconsin.

"Hey Chuck, are you up to some company?" Ken called from the porch.

A man who closely resembled Ken, only older with more weathered skin, opened the door for them. "What are you doing way out here? Are you slumming?"

"Not really. You know how Norman is, he brought home another stray. This is Jeff Cooper. Norman ran into him at the falls. You're not going to believe this, but he's the grandson of Tom Red Fox and his uncle is David Red Fox. Since you're planning the pow-wow for this weekend, I was hoping you wouldn't mind an extra overnight guest on Saturday night?"

"Come on in out of the heat and we'll talk about it. Jen is down at the community center getting ready for the weekend, but I think I can find us something cold to drink in the refrigerator. As for your question, you know there's always room for more. Norman and Hanna are planning to stay with Toby and his family, so I'll have plenty of room for you and Jeff. That is unless Jeff would prefer to stay with someone closer to his own age. I heard my grandsons are setting up a bachelor's lodge this year."

Jeff seated himself in a comfortable chair in the living room of the small house. It amazed him how comfortable he felt here. He took a minute to think about the proposal. He'd heard all the old stories about how the young unmarried men lived together in a lodge set aside for them. He often wondered what it would have been like to live the life of his ancestors.

He wished his grandfather had taken him to the pow-wows, but the old man insisted his studies were more important. Even though Uncle David went to several pow-wows, he'd never been invited to accompany him. It made him wonder if his family was as shamed by his white blood as Grandfather Cooper had been by his Native American heritage.

"I think I'd enjoy spending time in the bachelor's lodge - that is if they don't mind sharing space with a half breed."

"I have a feeling your grandparents sheltered you. Those young men all have some white blood somewhere in their past. You will be more than welcome."

Jeff smiled, then another thought popped into his mind. "Maybe we should skip going to Rapid City and seeing the monuments. I really should have my car here so I can take off for Montana on Monday morning."

Ken seemed to be deep in thought for a moment. "Did you leave your keys with Norman?"

"You know I did, just in case they had to move the car for any reason. Why do you ask?"

"Do you mind if Norman drives your car out here and then rides back with me?"

"That would be great. I really wanted to see the monuments with you rather than alone. I've discovered on this trip, it's a lot more interesting to share the things I see with someone else. Being an 'only' child, I've had my fill of solitude."

"The boy speaks like a wise old man," Chuck observed. "Are you following in your grandfather's footsteps? Are you a shaman?"

"Hardly. It's more like I'm following in my parent's footsteps. I'm going to Montana to be a high school teacher on the Blackfoot reservation. I know my parents made a difference on our reservation. I pray I can do the same for the people I am going to serve."

"Jeff is being too modest," Ken said. "While we were at one of the waysides, he made contact with his Spirit Guide. I was privileged to be allowed to witness it. It was an experience I won't soon forget."

"As well you shouldn't," Chuck commented. "I've never heard of such a thing happening." He turned his attention to Jeff. "Have you spoken with your Spirit Guide before? When did you go on your vision quest?"

"I didn't go on a quest as a young man. It's not a practice where I come from. This came as a complete surprise. I'm still trying to comprehend it all."

"Do you feel comfortable enough with it to tell me of your Spirit Guide?"

Jeff contemplated his answer. He certainly wasn't comfortable with what happened to him earlier, but not talking about it would only allow the questions in his mind to fester. "I had a vision of a great eagle, only not one like any I'd ever seen in the past. Instead of the feathers I'm used to seeing, his feathers were a blue grey in color. He told me my *man* name was going to be Blue Eagle Feather. I honestly don't know what to make of it. I never put much stock in such things, until it happened to me. I know I have a lot to digest, but Ken tells me when I get to my destination I should look for a man by the name of Alan Turtle."

A wide grin filled Chuck's face. "Ken's right. What you've described is something Alan would be able to interpret for you. He's one of the best. While the eagle is sacred to most of the people, the color blue is especially so to the Blackfoot."

Unlike when the vision first filled his conscious being, Jeff felt more at ease with the happenings of just hours earlier.

* * * *

After spending the night with Chuck and Jan, Jeff and Ken left for the tourist area around Deadwood, Custer and Rapid City. Jeff was anxious to see the monuments not only in Rapid City but also in Custer.

Before doing any sightseeing, they checked into the motel where Ken made reservations for them for the next two nights.

To appease his white ancestry, the first stop they made was at Mount Rushmore. The enormity of the sculpture on the side of the mountain was awe-inspiring. With his love of history, the faces of the presidents depicted on the mountain brought on a flood of emotions. Each of these men had done so much for this great country; he was inspired by this enormous art project sprawling before him.

"I can't imagine the amount of work that went into carving this into the mountain," he commented as they stood staring at the huge heads depicted on the rock wall.

"If you think this is something, wait until we get to Custer and you see Crazy Horse. I agree this was a massive undertaking, but the work on Crazy Horse is being done by a single man and his family. They are the true artists in this area. Of course, I'm prejudiced because Crazy Horse is one of my own people."

"I didn't mean to take anything away from the monument to one of the most talked about heroes of Native American history. I guess I'm torn between my white blood and that of my mother's people."

"I would be disappointed in you if you weren't torn," Ken replied. "It is my hope our time together on this journey will be productive for both sides of your heritage. Even though I am not qualified to try and explain the vision you experienced at the wayside, I feel you are destined to do great things for both of the cultures that have formed your background."

Jeff contemplated Ken's words as they drove the short distance between Mount Rushmore and Custer. As they drove, he poured over the information in the brochure he'd picked up, telling about the Crazy Horse Monument that was taking shape on the face of the enormous rock face of one of the area's mountains.

After pulling into the visitor's area, Jeff felt something akin to a spiritual awakening fill his being. The only thing he could compare it with was the way he felt when he stood at the Wounded Knee memorial at Pine Ridge.

I fought for our people, for your people. The whites tried to overrun us and unfortunately, they won. You have a calling in this life. Teach our children well. Help them to understand the way to live with the whites, is through education. You are destined to lead our people into the future. Lead them well and embrace the roots of both of your cultures.

The voice sounding within his head could have only belonged to the legendary Crazy Horse. This journey from Wisconsin into the land once ruled by the Sioux, Cheyenne, Blackfoot and others was becoming more complicated than he ever expected.

Once they stood on the viewing platform, he marveled at the beauty and complexity of the work being done on the monument. The details in the face rivaled that of the work he'd seen earlier in the day at Mount Rushmore. Although the finished product was years from completion, he

39

could visualize what it might look like in the future.

"Seeing this is very moving, isn't it?" Ken asked.

"It most certainly is. I can't even imagine the vision of the man who started this project. I doubt I would ever be able to think of doing such a thing by looking at that rock face."

"I completely agree. The only answer I can come up with is the man who started this as his lifelong work, was inspired by the ancestors. Am I wrong in thinking you heard the voices of the ancestors when we first arrived in the parking lot?"

"I heard a voice within my head. I know it's mind boggling, but I think it might have been Crazy Horse. I'm not quite sure what it meant, but I did heed what he had to say. I might have to rethink my lesson plans when I arrive in Montana."

"What do you mean? I guess I don't even know what you will be teaching."

Jeff smiled. "I'm trained to be a high school history teacher. The history I'm most familiar with is that of the whites, but I think I need to do more studying on that of the Native Americans from this area."

"I think the library of the College at Pine Ridge will be of a great help to you. It will be a boon to the young people of your classes to learn not only what the white man wants taught, but what comprises their own history as well."

Jeff thought long and hard on everything he'd learned over the past couple of days. Even the trip to Deadwood and the visit to the graveside to Wild Bill Hitchcock didn't rival the events he'd experienced at Crazy Horse and the Wounded Knee Memorial.

After spending the night in Rapid City, he was more than anxious to get back to Pine Ridge and the resources of the library the College maintained.

Chapter Five

Jeff found the library at the College more than helpful. He took the time to copy several articles and passages of books for things he could incorporate into his lesson plans.

He'd just finished his research when a young man came up to him in the library. "Are you Jeff Cooper?"

"That's me. I don't think I've had the pleasure."

The young man chuckled. "I'm Aaron Hawk. My grandfather told me you might be interested in sharing the bachelor quarters with us."

"He suggested it the other day when we were here. I've never done anything like this before. I'd like to experience it. Of course, you and your friends would have the last word on it. I'm the outsider here."

Aaron laughed. "That's not what Grandfather told me. He says you've been on a vision quest. I thought that was old school. I haven't heard of anyone going on a vision quest in years."

"I didn't *go* on a vision quest. It was more like the visions *came* to me."

"Visions? As in more than one?"

"Something like that. I just think it's my mind playing tricks on me, but Ken and your grandfather keep telling me it's more than that. They both say I'll learn more when I get to Montana and meet with Alan Turtle. For now, I just want to enjoy the pow-wow."

Aaron slapped Jeff on the back. "Since that's the case, come along with me. If you plan to stay in the bachelor's quarters with us, you have to help erect the lodge. Grandfather says it's one way for us to understand what life was like for our ancestors."

Jeff agreed. On the reservation where he'd grown up there was a symbolic teepee, but no one ever stayed in it. Instead of being made of buffalo hides, it was made of cement and meant mostly for the tourists. Considering it was placed outside of the visitor's center, it was more of a joke with the young people than anything connected with their history and the past.

The other young men were gathered in an open field that Aaron explained would be used for the ceremonies. Although they wore cut offs and tee shirts, it wasn't hard to visualize them as warriors of old. Unlike Ken and Norman, many of them wore their long hair in braids. For a moment, Jeff was transported back in time. He was no longer a teacher on his way to his first assignment. Instead, he became a warrior, erecting his lodge after roaming the prairie in search of the buffalo. Those around him became his fellow warriors and when a young woman joined them, she became an Indian maiden come to help the men with their project.

"This is Jeff Cooper," Aaron said as he started making the introductions. "He's from Wisconsin and is on his way to Montana and the Blackfeet Reserve. He's going to teach out there."

"I heard you were here," one of the young men said. "Is it true you had a vision of your Spirit Guide?"

"It was no big deal," Jeff replied. Even though he knew he'd had a life changing experience, he didn't want his time here to revolve around the one thing in his life he didn't understand.

"I think it's a big deal," another young man said. "At the pow-wows I hear a lot of older men talking about going on their vision quests. I thought that was a thing of the past. I mean, anymore. Our people don't change their names because they get older. I think it's rather sad we've lost that part of our heritage. Do you think any of us could go on a vision quest?"

"I'm hardly the one to ask," Jeff protested. "I don't understand what I experienced. Therefore, I can't begin to tell you if these things are real or dreams. I think it's something for each person to find for themselves."

"I agree with Jeff," Aaron said, coming to his rescue. "We've got work to do in setting up this lodge and then we can have fun at the pow-wow. If any of us have a spiritual experience this weekend, so much the better, but I know I've been enjoying these celebrations of our heritage all my life and I doubt this year will be any different."

Jeff was pleased that Aaron's statement silenced the young men's questions and tabled the discussion. He was relieved to realize his companions knew exactly what they were doing. If any of them were to ask him what to do next, he would be hard put to come up with an answer. Thankfully, they told him what to do and since it made sense, he did it willingly.

* * * *

By Friday afternoon, people began arriving from all over the country. Drum groups arrived and assessed the area where they would be performing. With Aaron as his companion and instructor for what was going on during the pow-wow, he learned how each drum group had a lead singer and all of the songs, although they each might sound the same, had different meanings.

"What are you wearing for the ceremonies tomorrow?" Aaron asked.

"Can't I wear this?"

"Hardly. When Grandfather said you hadn't been to a pow-wow before, I went through some of my regalia and found something for you to wear."

"Oh, I couldn't take your clothes."

"Why not? I've been working on new leggings and shirts over the winter. I've grown a lot since I wore some of these outfits and I don't mean in height. I got engaged this year and I think she's trying to show me what a good cook she is." He patted his expanding midsection to prove his point. "That said, I figured I deserved some new outfits. Come on over to the house and you can decide which ones you want to wear."

"Ones? As in more than one?"

"You've got a lot to learn, Jeff. I usually wear two to three different outfits during a pow-wow. I've got several different pair of leggings with tops to go with them and of course moccasins. There are also some headdresses, but I think Grandfather has something special for you to wear. At least that's what he said. When we finish at my place we're to go over to see him."

While at Aaron's home, Jeff tried on several different outfits before deciding on the two he planned to wear for the weekend. When he arrived at Chuck's place, he noticed his car parked out front, indicating that Norman and Hanna must have arrived.

"I wondered when we'd get to see the guest of honor for the pow-wow," Norman greeted him. "Have you found some regalia to wear?"

"Aaron loaned me something, although I could have gotten by wearing my own clothes. I'm not one of the dancers or anything."

"Is that what you think?" Jeff turned to see his Uncle David enter the room. "Norman called me and told me of your visions and how your Spirit Guide gave you your 'man' name. He said it will be celebrated this weekend, so your Aunt Betty and I made arrangements to fly out to Sioux Falls and come out here with them. I was the one who drove your car out here. It's a lot smaller than what I'm used to, but it does handle nicely. You made a good choice."

"I don't understand why these visions would be important to anyone but me."

Ken came to his side. "It's been a long time since someone of our people has experienced such vivid visions. I'm sure Aaron told you many of his friends have never gone on a vision quest. It's an old-fashioned idea and our people are moving forward, which is the way things should be. For you to have such a vision from your Spirit Guide is a momentous happening. Chuck and I have been planning to honor you at the pow-wow this weekend. While you have been with the young men, we have been working on a symbolic headdress for you."

Chuck went into another room of the house and came out with a headdress. It depicted an eagle with feathers trailing down on either side. Although the feathers were not the grey blue of the one tucked in Jeff's overnight bag, they were equally impressive.

"I don't know what to say. I'm afraid you're all making too much of this. We don't even know what any of this means."

"You'll learn," David said, putting his hand on Jeff's arm. "What happened to you is very special. Dad and I had a lot of talks about how many Native American traditions you should practice. I wanted you to go to the pow-wows with us, but Dad was adamant you needed to keep grounded in your white heritage. Welcome what has happened to you. Learn everything you can and embrace the culture you are entering."

* * * *

Saturday morning, Jeff watched the grand entrance, thrilled by the amount of history the regalia of the men and women who were dancing depicted. Headdresses ranged from headbands with feathers stuck in them to elaborate ones with coyote heads or those of other small animals, which had played such an important part in their history.

Some of the women wore dressed with bells sewed onto the skirts that tinkled when they walked and even more so when they danced. They made such a delicate sound they reminded Jeff of the songs of the birds.

He found the borrowed regalia from Aaron to be extremely comfortable. It was no wonder the ancestors enjoyed their leather garments over the stiff denim pants and cotton shirts of the white men. The natural leather seemed to breathe even more than the natural cotton fiber of his tee-shirt.

Even though he didn't understand the words of the songs, he soon was able to distinguish one from the other. Aaron even encouraged him to join the dancers in the sacred circle. It didn't take long for the drums to work their way into his soul and guided his feet in the same direction as the one taken by the other dancers.

In his mind, he traveled back over the years to a time when these people danced not for a pow-wow put on in a remembrance of the past, but for the sheer joy of dancing and rejoicing over the everyday occurrences in their lives.

The dance ended, but his mind remained active. He saw warriors seated on magnificent horses riding to war or going on the hunt for the food to supply their daily needs.

You are being allowed a glimpse of the past, the voice of the blue eagle from his earlier vision sounded within his head. *You are charged with keeping the past alive for those you will be going to serve. They need to know the history of their people as well as that of the whites. Listen to the elders and learn all they have to impart to you.*

As for why I have come to you, the great shaman of the Blackfoot people will be able to explain much to you. Even though you carry the blood of the whites, your heart is that of a noble warrior. You will be a great leader for the people.

"Are you all right, Jeff?" David's question silenced the voice he now equated with his Spirit Guide.

"Yes, I'm fine. I was just carried away by the beat of the music." He decided it was best if he kept the true reason for his trancelike state a secret known only to himself. Until he knew more about this gift he'd received from his Spirit Guide, he thought it best if he play things close to his chest.

David looked at him skeptically. He knew that look. He'd get it every time his uncle caught him in a lie or perhaps even a half truth. "Whatever you say. Personally I think there's more to it than you're saying, but I won't press you for something you're not willing to talk about."

"I appreciate it, Uncle David. I'm not sure about what is going on right now. As soon as I know more, you know I'll let you know."

"To be honest, Jeff, I've seen the look you had on your face before. It was when your grandfather, my dad, would go into a trance to communicate with the spirits. I didn't think things like this happened anymore. I've trained all my life to be a shaman, but I've never gone into a trance. I don't know if I should tell you what you're going through is a blessing or a curse." He emphasized his statement with a knowing wink.

Jeff nodded. He knew it was foolish to try and pull anything over on his uncle. Now that Grandfather was gone, David was the one and only person in the world who knew him the best.

With the trance broken, Jeff concentrated on the dancers as well as the chants of the drum circles. It didn't take long for the words of the songs along with the beat of the drum to bring on the trancelike state again.

Before his mind's eye, a village of the Sioux materialized. It looked like many of the ones he'd seen depicted in the Hollywood movies about the Native American tribes. The tipis made from the hides of the buffalo looked as if they'd sprung up from the prairie like strange looking plants. As the vision clarified, he saw the homes of the ancestors scattered in a circular pattern across the prairie with all the entrances facing to the East.

The rising sun is very important to the people. Always remember to face the east as you begin your day. Pay homage to the sun, for it is the sun that rules our lives. While you are with the Sioux, learn all you can about the Sun Dance. The whites never understood the reason for this ceremony. The spiritual rebirth of those who participated is the importance of the Sun Dance. The whites saw this as barbaric. The ancients saw it as a religious experience.

As soon as he heard the voice, he saw a vision of a young warrior preparing to sacrifice his body. Seeing the medicine man pierce the young man's skin to insert the bone skewer seemed as natural as taking communion in church on Sunday morning. He watched in awe as the skewer was attached to a long rope and the man was lifted into the air to hang until he could free himself from the skewer.

Inwardly, Jeff could feel the pain as the ceremony not only began, but also went on for an excruciatingly long time. When at last the young man broke free of the skewers and fell to earth, Jeff monitored his feelings and felt the rebirth of his being just as the man in his vision did.

"Are you ready to get something to eat?"

Aaron's question shattered the vision and brought Jeff back to the present and the events going on around him. "Eat?"

"Where were you? I know you're with us physically, but where was your mind?"

Jeff shook his head. "I'm afraid you don't want to know. What's on the menu?"

Aaron winked broadly. "Would you believe me if I said puppy stew and fry bread?"

Jeff rolled his eyes. "I think I've had this conversation before, like when I was in Sioux Falls. Now what are we really having?"

"Bar-b-que and fry bread but I don't think you've ever had bar-b-que like this before. It's made with venison."

Jeff laughed at the comment. "Where do you think I've been all my life? I was brought up on a reservation in Northern Wisconsin. My grandfather and uncle went hunting every fall, and until I went to college, I ate more venison than beef. It will be like having a family dinner at home."

Pangs of hunger gnawed at Jeff's stomach. He knew he needed nourishment, but he also wanted to know the fate of the young warrior in his vision. As he thought of what he'd seen in his mind, he realized his chest hurt as though the skewers had been ripped from his skin and left him with the pain of rebirth.

* * * *

After eating lunch, Jeff sought out Ken and Chuck. He had to share his experience with someone but knew it couldn't be either his Uncle David or Aaron. He found the Hawk brothers relaxing at the far end of the pavilion.

"Are you enjoying the pow-wow, Jeff?" Charles asked.

"It's been very moving. I know the two of you play an important part in today's festivities, but when and if you have time, I'd like to talk to you."

"You sound serious," Ken remarked. "With the lunch break, we have time now. Why don't we go over to Chuck's place where we can talk privately?"

Jeff breathed a sigh of relief and followed the two older men away from the celebration grounds to Chuck's home.

"David talked to me earlier and we've been watching you intently," Ken began once they were alone behind closed doors. "If I'm not mistaken, you're having more visions like the ones you experienced earlier."

Jeff nodded, amazed at how many people were aware of what was happening to him, more and more, as he traveled west to his new position. He took a deep breath before he revealed the visions he'd seen during the dancing of the morning.

Once Jeff finished relating the visions, no one spoke for a moment. "I'd give anything to have seen what you did today. I've heard of the Sun Dance, but of course those were done in the past."

"I could even feel the pain of the young warrior I watched during the Sun Dance," Jeff confessed.

"Where did you feel the pain?"

Jeff put both hands over his chest where he'd seen the skewers placed in his vision.

"Interesting," Ken said. "Would you mind taking off your shirt?"

The request bewildered Jeff, but he made no comment. Instead, he pulled the shirt over his head. To his surprise, the place where he felt the pain showed two scabbed over scars. Even though he hadn't participated in the Sun Dance, his body now bore the scars. In the past, this would have been a badge of honor, but in the twenty-first century, how could he

48

explain them?

Both Chuck and Ken stared at the scars and remained speechless for several seconds. "You felt the pain," Ken said, "because the young warrior was you in a previous life. You are blessed to have been given a glimpse of the past and I'm sure it will not be the last one you will receive."

"How can this be? I have Native American blood, but it's Chippewa. How could I have been a Sioux warrior in another life?"

Chuck laughed at the question. "You may have a college education, Jeff, but you have so much more to learn. In the present day, we have learned we are all brothers rather than members of tribes who are at war with each other. Maybe it was the birth of the white buffalo that bound us together. Whatever it was, we are grateful to the ancestors for bringing the nations together. I think the knitting together of the people is just beginning. You will be the key to the future."

Jeff contemplated all he'd heard from Ken and Chuck. He didn't want to be the key to anything. All he wanted was to be a history teacher and to help kids growing up on a reservation in the same way his parents did before their deaths.

* * * *

Jeff realized he had a lot to think over and the commotion of the pow-wow was not the place to do it. Rather than dwell on what was happening in his life, he immersed himself in the celebration. He even sought out the old men and women. He asked each of them if they could tell him stories of the past.

Some of the people related stories much like the ones Jeff heard from his grandfather all his life. Others told stories of the atrocities the whites did against the Native Americans no matter what the tribe. Although he'd heard whispered conversations about such things, they were not taught in any of his college history courses.

Saturday evening the dancing, songs and storytelling went far into the night. By the time Jeff returned to the bachelor's lodge, his head was so full of everything he learned throughout the day, he found sleep a reluctant visitor. Once he did fall asleep, he dreamed of the people of the past. As each scene played out in Jeff's subconscious, he recalled one of the stories he'd heard from the elders at the pow-wow.

The stories told to you by the elders are true. Remember them well and do not let your students forget their history. The future of our people depends on the education of the young.

Jeff awoke with a start and sat up expecting to see the giant blue eagle hovering over where he slept. Instead of the image of the Spirit Guide he expected, he was greeted by the sleeping forms of the young men he now called friends as well as their contented snores.

Am I ever going to be able to sleep peacefully without such troubling dreams?

To his surprise, the voice of his Spirit Guide resonated within the confines of his mind.

You have been chosen for a reason. The scars of the Sun Dance on your chest are proof of the choices made by the ancients. Sleep well my son. I promise you will get the rest you need, but do not forget your dreams and visions.

With those words still echoing in Jeff's subconscious, he drifted off into a peaceful sleep.

* * * *

Jeff awoke to the sounds of morning as his friends prepared to start the new day. For the first time since he experienced his first vision in Sioux Falls, he felt fully rested.

"What's on the agenda for today, Aaron?" Jeff asked once he got up.

"We start out by a cleansing swim in the river. Once we're clean, and dressed, we will be attending Sunday services. I think you'll find it quite interesting as several of the hymns are written in the language of not only the plains tribes, but also those of some of the eastern tribes as well."

"A cleansing swim?" David questioned, as though he hadn't heard the remainder of what Aaron said. "Why not a hot shower?"

Aaron laughed. "For this weekend we live as our ancestors lived. They didn't have hot showers but contrary to the belief of the whites, weren't 'dirty savages.' Unlike the whites who came to conquer them, they bathed daily in the river. I have to admit, I wouldn't want to do something like that when the weather starts to get cold, but I do enjoy a morning swim in the summer."

Jeff agreed. He'd always known of the cleanliness of the Native Americans, but he'd never considered skinny-dipping in an open river in the light of day. Maybe he'd do it at night, but this was morning and the sun had already risen over the eastern horizon.

He followed Aaron and the others down to the river, where the other men attending the pow-wow had gathered to greet the morning. The older men took ceremonial baths while the younger ones whooped and hollered as they jumped into the waters of the lazy flowing river.

Jeff did as the others and ran into the water until the channel became deep and they dove beneath the water to begin swimming. When he'd been in high school, he'd gone skinny dipping one night after a party at the high school. Unlike today, the moon had been the only light illuminating the night. Today, the rising sun showed the sleek bronze bodies of his companions.

Even without the visions he'd been plagued with for the past few days, he knew the ritual of young men bathing together in this river was an age-old custom. It took little time for Jeff to become one with his companions and to forget that at any moment, one of the women or children might come upon the naked men.

The giggles from the bank brought Jeff back to the present. Several young women stood watching the men swimming in the river. He was relieved to think these women would see only a man naked from the waste up, with the remainder of his body concealed by the water. They were lucky their antics had stirred up the silt from the bottom, making the water more murky than usual.

At last, the women left, and the men got out of the water to grab their towels. The natural act made Jeff wonder how the ancestors dried their bodies after their morning swim.

The thought of allowing the air to dry his naked body made him shiver at the very thought of it. It was entirely possible the ancients were more liberal when it came to nudity. It was something he needed to talk to someone about, but not these young men who shared the bachelor's lodge with him. He was certain if he mentioned it, they would think he was a bit of a prude.

"Exhilarating, isn't it?" Aaron asked. "I should have warned you about the girls coming down to spy on us."

"Do you think the same thing happened to the ancestors?"

"Sure I do. People don't change. Girls are girls no matter where they live in history. Of course, back then, there was no mystery to be solved concerning the bodies of men and women. Life was different back then. Whole families lived in a lodge together and the sex act was nothing secretive or taboo to talk about. It was natural."

Jeff laughed; his nervous thoughts of moments earlier seemed to disappear. "You must have read my mind."

Now it was Aaron's turn to be the one to laugh. "I remember the first time I was old enough to take the morning swim. I was self-conscious about being nude in the river and maybe having one of the girls see me. At the time, I had an older friend who told me pretty much what I just told you. I was about fifteen at the time and since then I've come to enjoy the early morning swim. Come back next year and it will seem like the most natural thing to do, even with the girls trying to see more than they should."

By the time they returned to the bachelor's lodge and dressed for the day, Aaron said they needed to get over to the ceremonial grounds for the Sunday services.

Jeff was joined by his Uncle David as well as Norman, Ken, and Chuck. It came as a surprise when Hannah and Betty weren't with them. "Where are the women?" he asked.

"They'll be here shortly," David assured him. "You know your Aunt Betty has a beautiful voice. She's been singing in the church choir back home ever since she was a kid. It's the same with Hannah. They usually lead the hymn sing."

He'd no more than said the words before several women joined the growing congregation. Once they passed out the copies of the hymns they would be singing, the two of them waited for the presider to begin the service.

Although Jeff was certain the ancients didn't have organized religious services like the one being played out today, he knew they were just as devoted to the worship of their gods as the Christians of today were.

When the singing began, he immediately recognized the tunes to the old hymns that were being sung to such foreign words. Even though he couldn't understand the words, Jeff was able to at least hum along with the tune.

The words of the proclamation were meaningful. The speaker said it was the modern day duty of all Native Americans to be accepting to everyone and strive to do their best for the people.

"Good message," David said as they greeted the speaker. "You said it all."

"What did you think of our service, Jeff?" Norman asked.

"It was different, but in a way very much like any other I've attended. At least the main topic wasn't about money."

His statement brought a laugh from his friends.

"I've been to services like that," Chuck confessed. "I was speaking at a conference in Casper, Wyoming and my hosts asked me to accompany them to church. I have to admit the pastor was a good speaker, but when he asked for someone to come to the parsonage and wash the kitchen floor for his wife, he lost me."

"You're making that up, Uncle Chuck," Norman accused.

"I swear it's the truth. This guy thought, since the church owned the parsonage, they should do the heavy duty cleaning, like floor washing. I could have understood if he told the congregation the parsonage needed a new roof, but I thought he was completely out of line. After the service, I got a good look at the pastor's wife. She was what you could call a trophy wife and I'm sure she thought she might break a nail or something."

Jeff tried to imagine his pastor back home making such a request and admitted he couldn't even envision such a thing.

Chapter Six

After partaking in another buffet type lunch, the opening ceremonies for the final day of the pow-wow began.

Unlike the day before when Jeff watched the dancers in awe, he joined with his friends in the first dance around the sacred circle. After his vision of the Sun Dance, he felt the music deep in his soul. Each beat of the drums now had special meaning for him.

By three o'clock, people were beginning to pack up their cars for the drive home. Jeff found it hard to say good-bye to his uncle for the second time in a month.

"I really wasn't planning to come to this pow-wow, but when Norm contacted me to say he'd met you and was sure you were going to stay for this, I couldn't stay away. I wish Dad was here to see the change in you."

"Have I changed that much?"

"You know you have. The visions you've been experiencing are ones he would understand much more than I do. When you got your scholarship with the stipulation you teach on a reservation for five years, he said you would find your roots. I will be interested in hearing what the shaman on the Blackfoot reservation has to say about them."

Jeff smiled. "I don't know if I'm as excited about this as you are. To be truthful, I'm more frightened about it than anything else. The visions I've had over the past few days have, at times, been downright terrifying."

David pulled him into a bear hug. "Embrace your heritage and allow your Spirit Guide to show you the path your life should take."

Jeff pondered his uncle's words as he hugged his aunt and waved until they rounded the curve and drove out of sight.

"When will you be leaving for Montana?" Chuck asked, once most of the people from out of the area left for home.

"I thought I'd leave tomorrow morning. Since I'm in no hurry, I thought I'd like to see Yellowstone, The Little Big Horn, and Glacier National Park."

"Would you mind having some company for the trip?"

Jeff looked at Chuck, wondering what he was suggesting. He had to admit, he'd enjoyed seeing South Dakota with Ken, but would he be as comfortable with Chuck? "What are you thinking?"

"I've been promising Aaron I'd take him to see many of the areas you're going to visit. I also said I'd take him to see Chief Plenty Coups State Park and the Indian Caves State Park up by Billings. We'd be able to help you out with gas and lodging. Once you get settled, you could take us to Helena so we could get a flight home."

Jeff thought for only a minute before agreeing to Chuck's proposal. With everything he'd experienced since arriving in South Dakota, it wouldn't hurt to have the old shaman with him. He also knew he would enjoy taking the trip with Aaron. Trips like these were always better when shared with friends.

* * * *

By seven o'clock on Monday morning, Jeff and his passengers were packed and ready to leave. They hoped to be at Yellowstone by nightfall, and made reservations for one of the rustic cabins the park offered.

Upon check in, they were pleased to have plenty of room, and were within walking distance of many of the overlooks as well as the geysers. Jeff took several pictures and wondered if the Native Americans in this area were as impressed with the beauty of the park as the many visitors who came to marvel at it.

"Do you know any stories about this area?" he finally asked Chuck.

"I've heard the ancients were afraid of the geysers, but that's just a myth. I've done a lot of research on it and this area has been inhabited since twelve thousand years ago. I like to think it was the abundance of game animals as well as the hot springs that brought people to this area."

Jeff thought about the ancients. He wished he would get a glimpse of what their lives were like. As soon as the thought popped into his head, he realized he'd become greedy. While the visions were frightening at first, now he wanted more.

"I take it you haven't had any visions of the people who lived here," Aaron commented.

"No I haven't, but I have a feeling I'm being greedy. Anything I can learn will help me in my lesson planning. I know what I'm supposed to be teaching in my history classes, but I'm coming to think I should be learning more about the history of my heritage. I'm afraid these stories are being lost to the kids growing up on the reservations today."

Chuck nodded sagely. "You're right. Our history is being lost to the young. They have other things to occupy their time, especially the Internet, their smart phones, and all those other electronic gadgets they're always using."

Aaron looked up from his phone. "It's not that bad, Grandpa. I just use my phone to keep in touch with my friends."

"And to play games," Jeff added. "I understand what Chuck is saying. It's not just the kids on the reservations that are hooked on these things. I don't know how many kids I saw texting or playing games when they should have been listening to the lectures in class. It was tempting, but I never fell into that trap. The way I saw it, I was at the University to get a degree, not to play Angry Birds or whatever other game was popular at the time."

Embarrassment was mirrored in Aaron's eyes. "I guess you're right." He quickly closed his phone. "From here on in, I'll only be checking my phone at night."

Jeff watched as Aaron sipped the phone into his pocket. He wondered if Aaron would be able to keep from checking the phone at regular intervals. It was doubtful, but time would tell.

* * * *

The next morning, they prepared to check out the wonders of the park. After breakfast at the main lodge, they marveled at the sight of Old Faithful erupting right on schedule. From there, they drove around the park and enjoyed the view from several different overlooks.

Upon seeing a herd of buffalo grazing on an open prairie, Jeff experienced a vision of a band of hunters lying in wait for the shaggy beasts. In the vision, it soon became apparent, the people he saw were ancients. There were no horses in sight and the hunters ran on foot to force the herd over one of the bluffs to fall to their deaths.

As the vision progressed, he watched as the hunters along with several women rushed to the bottom of the bluffs to finish off the lives of the dazed beasts and harvest the meat for consumption by the people of their village. The gore of the blood from the dead animals seemed to consume the vision. Soon everything became tinged in red before a darkness overcame Jeff, ending the vision and rendering him unconscious.

"Jeff, Jeff."

Conscious thought returned to Jeff's mind as he felt Aaron tapping his cheeks as he called his name. "Wh-what happened?" he managed to ask.

"I don't know," Aaron confessed. "We were standing here watching the buffalo herd and then you went all quiet. The next thing I knew, you passed out."

The vision became vivid in his memory, but he didn't want to tell Aaron or even Chuck about it. Even though Aaron was the grandson of a great shaman, he doubted the young man would understand. As for Chuck, he had been the one to say it was best to talk to Alan Turtle, the great shaman on the Blackfoot reservation. Perhaps he could make sense of the visions he'd been experiencing ever since he crossed the state line from Minnesota to South Dakota.

Jeff gazed up at the sky in the hopes he could come up with a plausible reason for losing consciousness. The day was indeed warm and with the sun already past its zenith, he knew exactly what he was going to say.

"I think it must be the heat, combined with being way past lunch time. I was so excited to see the park, I didn't eat much at breakfast. Let's go back down to the lodge. We can have a late lunch and get something cool to drink."

Even though the excuse sounded a bit lame to Jeff, Aaron and Chuck seemed to buy it. It didn't take them long to get down to the lodge and order sandwiches along with tall glasses of iced tea. They ate in silence, giving Jeff time to think about the true reason for his unconscious state.

In his mind, he could feel the adrenalin rush brought on by the chase of the buffalo until they were forced over the bluff where they fell to their death. He'd read about such hunts in history class, but to actually see it, and become one with the hunters came as a complete surprise.

Was I one of those hunters in a prior life?

The thought crossing his mind went against everything he'd ever learned in church. As a Christian, he certainly didn't believe in reincarnation. Yet how else could he explain the scars that appeared on his chest after the vision of the Sun Dance?

If he was reincarnated from the Sioux warrior in his vision, why was he born Chippewa? Another question was, if he was reincarnated from one of the ancient hunters, to what tribe did they belong? Had the Sioux once hunted in the area of the Yellowstone or were the hunters he saw in his vision of one of the other tribes of the plains?

"You passing out was more than just the sun or hunger, wasn't it?"

Chuck's question came as a surprise. "What are you talking about?"

"I saw the look on your face when you experienced the vision about the Sun Dance. I saw that same look today. Did you have another vision?"

Jeff knew he couldn't tell a lie. "I did, but I don't know what to make of it. I hope you don't mind if I don't tell you about it until I can talk to the shaman at the reservation."

Aaron smiled. "If it was me, I'd be reluctant to say anything as well. To be truthful, I'd be scared shitless and I grew up with this stuff."

Chuck reached across the table and took Jeff's hand. "I understand what Aaron means. It was hard for me to accept the role of shaman, even though I'd trained for it all my life. Ken took to it like a duck to water, but I questioned my destiny. How much did your grandfather tell you about the people?"

Jeff thought for a moment before answering. "I was brought up knowing about the history of the Native American people, but Grandfather didn't push me to take part in any of the pow-wows. He knew my father's white blood needed to be acknowledged along with the heritage of my mother. I wish I would have been more attentive to all the

58

things he was telling me. It certainly would have helped me understand what's going on in my life."

"You don't talk much about your dad. What was he like?" Chuck asked.

"I was quite young when my parents were killed. I learned more about him on the day I graduated from college and met his sister, and then his brother. They insisted I meet their father, but it was a less than impressive meeting. I knew he'd disowned my father because of his marriage to my mother. Age hasn't mellowed the old man. I'm glad I won't ever have to deal with him again."

Aaron shook his head. "What a shame. I've always been taught to honor the elders, no matter what their temperament. What did your grandfather have to say about your meeting?"

"Grandfather had many visions and knew before I even returned home what I'd found when I met with my paternal grandfather. I think he was saddened by the way the old man treated me. He always tried to shield me from the prejudices of the outside world. Of course, at college, I was on my own, but I never had any problems. The university in Madison is so diversified; no one gave my heritage much thought. I was just one of the guys at the dorm."

Talking about the day he graduated, made Jeff think about the events that changed his opinion of his white family. His whole life was spreading out in front of him and the last thing he wanted was to find the family who shunned his father for so many years. The realization his friends Karl and Jenny were in some way related, was almost too much to comprehend.

Thinking about his friends made him realize Jenny's aunt and uncle, which were also his aunt and uncle, would be attending their wedding. In light of everything he'd experienced since crossing over into South Dakota, he wondered how he would react to the white side of his family. At this moment, he felt more connected to his Native American heritage than anything in the white world.

"Tomorrow we will be crossing over into Montana," Chuck said, changing the course of the conversation. "Are you worried about going to the memorial at the Little Big Horn? I've been there several times and it always saddens me to think the whites put up a memorial to Yellow

Hair, but not one to those of our people who also gave their lives that day."

Jeff nodded. "I've watched several documentaries on the Little Big Horn. I've seen a couple of ones from the Native American point of view and even one about a man who said he rode away from the battle and lived to tell about it. It's hard to know what to believe. I put a lot more credence to the accounts from the people in the Native American version."

"I remember when they filmed the documentary," Chuck commented. "It was one of the old women from our reservation who spoke about how her father told her about how he participated in the battle. I grew up on those stories and when I was Aaron's age, I could hardly wait to make the trip to see the battleground. It was a place of sadness, but it still draws me like a powerful magnet. I also saw the documentary about the white man who says he survived. I know there was a lot of controversy over that one, but I tend to believe he was there. If he was, indeed, wounded, and rode away from the actual battle, it was possible the warriors paid him little attention. It's only my opinion, but I think the man the people wanted to see die was Yellow Hair. Many of the people thought he was crazy and that's the reason his body wasn't violated in the same way as his men. From the accounts of the elders, I know the people were whispering his name long before the actual battle took place. Unfortunately, for both sides, the fool walked into a trap with too few men to defend his position. For years after the battle, our people suffered at the hands of the whites who wanted revenge, even if it were on the women and children of undefended villages. Of course that's a story for another time and another place."

Jeff nodded his agreement. He remembered reading several books about how the army would attack villages early in the mornings when no one expected it. The one story that always stuck with him was that of Chief Black Kettle. He'd been a man of peace and taken his people to the Sand Creek Reservation. During the massacre of Sand Creek, Black Kettle survived, but his wife was shot several times. After that, he moved his people to Kansas. Above his tipi flew a white flag, but when Custer's men attacked just before dawn, they ignored the sign of peace. Both Black Kettle and his wife died on that day in 1868. It was no wonder the people hated Yellow Hair so much. If the man had no compassion for a man of peace who displayed a sign of his peaceful ways, it was possible he wanted to see the Native American people wiped off the face of the earth. His death was more than an act of revenge, it was a moral sentence that in the modern day world, would have been considered only right for a serial killer.

* * * *

The next morning, they pulled out of the park and stopped at a small filling station to fill up before driving across the state of Montana. While Aaron pumped the gas, Jeff went into the office to pay for their purchase and pick up a map.

The old man sitting behind the desk looked up as Jeff put the map as well as several snacks on the counter.

"Tourists?" the man inquired.

Jeff nodded. "I'm doing a little sightseeing before I start my new job next month."

"You should have been here a month ago. There was a snowdrift as high as this building right where your car is parked."

Jeff looked out across the parking lot. "So what do you do here in the winter? I mean if the snow was still piled high a month ago, you probably don't get much traffic around here."

The old man spit a stream of tobacco into a can he picked up from the desk before answering. "We leave. Me and the wife have a place down in Sun City. We much prefer the Arizona sunshine to the Montana blizzards." He laughed at his own joke. "Say, ain't you one of them Indians? Are you supposed to be off your reservation?"

Jeff glanced at the shotgun and rifle hanging on the gun rack on the wall behind the counter and weighed his answer carefully. With the man's comment, he'd been instantly transported back over a hundred years to when any Indian found off the reservation was shot on sight as a renegade. "Just been out in the sun a lot."

The man still eyed him skeptically as he rang up the purchases along with the cost of the gas and handed Jeff back his change. "Hope you enjoy your sightseeing in Montana."

"I will, thanks."

Once outside the small building, Jeff took a deep breath of the clear mountain air. "That was interesting," he said when he got back into the car. He was relieved Chuck was driving. His confrontation with the station attendant left him shaken.

"How often have you run into bigots who think all Indians should be confined to the reservations?"

Chuck started to laugh. "I take it you met Pete. He's run this station for the past forty years. I ran into him the first time I came to the park. He's a legend around here. Believe me, his bark is a lot worse than his bite. I actually got to know him. He loves to give people a hard time. I wouldn't have wanted to meet up with him a hundred years ago, but he's not a bad sort."

Jeff laughed nervously. "He had me spooked, especially when I saw those guns mounted on the wall behind the counter."

"I'll bet he's in there laughing his ass off for giving you a good scare," Chuck said. "I say we go back and talk to him. It would be good to see him again." He punctuated his comment with a wink.

Jeff turned in time to see not only the wink but also the sly smile crossing the older man's lips. "I think I'll pass on that one. Maybe another time."

Chuck was still laughing over Jeff's encounter with Pete as they turned toward Chief Plenty Coups State Park. As they drove toward their destination, Chuck told the story of the Crow chief who went to war and then pushed for peace. He even had a farm with his wife, Strikes The Iron, along with a general store, and at the time of his death, she insisted the farm should be made into a park.

Jeff marveled at the two-story log cabin where the revered chief and his wife lived and worked their farm, bridging the gap between the native people and the invading whites. As he read the literature and walked around the park, he realized there was so much Native American history that wasn't being taught, he wanted to learn more.

Reluctantly they left the park and headed to the site of the battle of the Little Bighorn. Here the atmosphere was completely different. This was a memorial not to a beloved chief, but to a monster who terrorized the tribes throughout the west. Unfortunately, it was also a memorial to the men who, as soldiers, were obliged to follow this mad man into a battle he could never win.

Rather than walk the area where the soldiers fell to the bullets and arrows of the assembled Indians, Chuck insisted they go to the staging area for the attack of the assembled warriors.

As if on cue, Jeff experienced a vision of the warriors waiting to attack the blue coats who were riding into their territory. He immediately recognized the young warrior who participated in the Sun Dance in his previous vision. If he was indeed the reincarnation of this man as Chuck suggested, he had been in the battle and perhaps even lost his life here.

The excitement of the anticipated battle overcame the feeling of dread filling Jeff's being. He could feel his muscles tensing as he waited for the moment the battle would begin. Like the adrenaline rush he'd experienced when he watched the ancient buffalo hunt only days earlier, he knew this was something he'd experienced in the past. In his mind, he was ready to charge into the valley below to destroy the men who not only terrorized his people, but also threatened the lifestyle his people enjoyed since the beginning of time.

War whoops filled his mind. They came from the assembled army of Native Americans, and echoed across the stillness of the July afternoon, and caused his heart to race with the excitement. The vision started to fade, but to Jeff's relief, he didn't lose consciousness. The quiet ridge and valley below became nothing more than a memorial to those who gave their lives on this very ground.

"I thought you might have a vision here. This is sacred ground, not only to the whites, but to us as well," Chuck said.

"I did and for the first time, I saw the battle from the point of view of the Indians who fought and died here. It's funny, as a kid, my friends and I would often play cowboys and Indians. Because of my white blood, I was always the white man who died from the pretend bullets and rubber tipped arrows. Today, I was one with the warriors who would wage battle with Custer and his men. I felt their excitement. It must have been an exhilarating victory. If only they could have seen the repercussions from their actions, maybe things would have been different for both sides."

"I never thought about it that way," Aaron commented. "Ma used to say, hindsight was always 20/20. Now we can see the mistakes made by both sides, but back then, they were only doing what they thought was right for them."

"You're right," Chuck added. "We wanted to keep our ancestral lands and the lifestyle we'd enjoyed since the beginning of time. The whites were hungry for not only land, but also the gold hidden in the hills of the west. Unfortunately, Hollywood romanticized the battles and made the Indians out to be the bad guys. This is an exciting time for us to be living in. Many of the predictions of the past are coming to pass and I think we will see things we never expected to see in our lifetime."

Jeff made no attempt to reply to Chuck's statement. Instead, he turned his thoughts inward and contemplated the ramifications of the visions he'd been having over the past several days.

* * * *

Before returning to Billings to spend the night, they made a stop at Indian Caves State Park. Since this was one of the places Chuck wanted to visit, Jeff saw no reason for not making the stop.

Here they saw the petroglyphs from the ancients. To Jeff's surprise, they triggered no new visions. It was extremely possible none of his previous incarnations were connected to this place.

For the second time, he pondered the meaning of the idea of reincarnation, which kept entering his mind. He was a Christian. He wasn't supposed to believe in such things. For some reason, he couldn't discount the visions he'd experienced as well as the scars on his chest resembling those of the ones left by the ritual of the Sun Dance.

Chapter Seven

From Billings, they took their time in getting to Helena. After dropping Aaron and Chuck off at the airport, he made his way to the address he had for Karl and Jenny's apartment.

For a young couple just starting out, it was larger than he expected, and not far from the hospital where Karl would be doing his internship.

"I see you found us," Karl greeted him when he answered the door.

"Those GPS thingies are a wonderful invention. I typed in your address and the sweet voice on the thing told me exactly where to go. I was wondering if I could crash here on your couch for a couple of nights. I'm not expected on the reservation until the first of next week."

"Couch? Hell, we have a second bedroom and you're more than welcome to say in there. For us it's nothing more than wasted space. When Jenny gets home, I'm sure she'll agree with me completely. Let's go out and get your stuff and get you settled."

Jeff admitted, if only to himself, he was looking forward to the time he would be able to spend with his old college roommate. At least here, he was certain he would be free of the visions that plagued him almost non-stop since he started his journey to the beginning of the rest of his life.

When Jenny returned to the apartment, Jeff insisted on taking everyone out to dinner so he wouldn't be a burden on his hosts.

Throughout the meal, Karl asked about his trip so far. After telling about his uneventful drive across Minnesota, he told them of the friends he'd made in South Dakota, and the thrill of being a part of the pow-wow even if he did have to borrow the regalia he wore for the event.

"It's a shame you don't have your own regalia. I met a gal here, and

65

that's what she does for a living. Since you'll be living on a reservation, you should have at least one outfit for the pow-wows you will be attending."

"I was thinking of doing that when I got settled. I'd like to be able to fit in with the people I'll be teaching. I do appreciate your offer, but I think my idea is the best. Besides, I was hoping I'd be able to spend some time with the two of you, and see what I could do to help with the wedding plans."

Jenny laughed at his statement. "Since when did you become a wedding planner? Somehow, I can't see you dealing with bakeries, florists, or any of the other people we need to talk to about the wedding. What you can do is get fitted for your tux. My mom and aunt are coming out next week to handle all the last minute things with Karl's mom. So you see, everything is under control. Since we knew you were coming, Karl was able to get the next couple of days off so the two of you can do something together."

"What about you? Don't you want to join us?"

"I've been busy doing the orientation at the hospital. I've got a physical scheduled for tomorrow, but the next day is wide open, so be sure to plan something I can participate in as well. I won't be starting work until a week from next Monday."

"I was thinking about the two of us going golfing tomorrow morning," Karl said. "You do have your clubs with you, don't you?"

"To be truthful I shipped then on ahead, but I'm sure I can either rent some or use yours. As I recall, we used to share clubs a lot when we were in school. At least until I was able to get my own set. It worked out well when we were in school, it should work well now."

"You've got me there, Buddy. I don't have a problem with sharing."

Jeff turned the conversation to Karl and Jenny's trip to Montana as well as their jobs.

"I have to admit the work as an intern is grueling," Karl said. "I'm lucky to get these two days off as well as the weekend of the wedding. I'm afraid it will be quite a while before we can have a real honeymoon."

"I think we already had the honeymoon," Jenny added. "We drove practically straight through to get here, and then went to Glacier National Park and treated ourselves to a really posh room at the Prince of Wales

Hotel for the three days before Karl had to start at the hospital. We knew his internship as well as his residency would be all work and very little play time."

Jeff envisioned the hotel Jenny was talking about. When he was at the park, he went in to see how the rich people lived and promptly deemed it was well beyond his means. "The Prince Of Wales Hotel is pretty expensive. How were you able to swing it?"

Karl smiled at the question. "I could hardly believe it when my grandparents offered us the three nights on them. It was our graduation present. Needless to say, they have the means and told us they knew the next few years would be hard for us. Grandpa is a doctor and Grandma is a lawyer. They both struggled when they were our age, and have been helping us out. They're even helping us with the rent on this place until Jenny can get established in her job. My dad is their only child just like I'm his only child. They said they wanted to see what we did with the inheritance that would be mine once they were gone."

Jeff pondered this new information about the man who had been his roommate for the entire time they were in school. Even though Jeff knew Karl was an only child, never once did he infer he had unlimited funds he could tap.

How different we are. I have a half way decent nest egg from the social security money Grandfather refused to touch, but there's no way he would have been able to subsidize me until I got on my feet.

* * * *

"You do realize I'm planning to beat your butt as usual," Karl joked as they prepared to tee off.

Jeff nodded. "So why should today be any different than any other time when we've played golf together? Golf is fun but I admit it's not *my* sport."

Karl laughed. "I know what you mean. Neither one of us is a pro, but getting out in the fresh air and enjoying time with a good friend is worth a million."

From the first swing, Jeff noticed something different in his game. Not only did he get par on every hole, he even managed to get a hole in one. He wondered what made today's game different from every other game he'd played against Karl for the past four years.

"What have you been doing, practicing behind my back?" Karl questioned after they completed the eighteenth hole.

"To be truthful, I haven't touched a club since we played just before graduation. With the funeral and everything we had to do afterwards, I was just too busy to even practice in the backyard. I guess I was having a good day today."

They both had a good laugh about Jeff's newfound golfing prowess as they made their way back to the apartment. Out of the blue, a thought popped into Jeff's head. He wondered if his expertise had anything to do with the strange visions he'd been having ever since he first stopped in South Dakota.

He gave the matter no further thought. These days were ones he planned to spend with his friends and not even think about his Spirit Guide or any of the other things he'd learned during his time with Ken and Chuck.

* * * *

The next morning, Jeff, Karl and Jenny went to the shop where the tuxedos had been ordered so Jeff could have his fitting before leaving for a day long road trip to explore the surrounding area.

"This is your country, Buddy," Jeff said as they pulled out onto the highway. "Where are you taking us?"

Karl took them on a tour of the capital city that was now their home. After lunch, they explored one of the national forests in the area before returning to the apartment in time for dinner.

Jeff insisted on buying steaks for the grill as well as some potatoes for baking. He'd been happy to find ones in plastic wrap in the produce department that could be baked in the microwave, keeping the prep time for dinner to a minimum.

"You didn't have to get all this stuff," Jenny protested as he took over her kitchen. "You took us out for dinner last night, and then lunch today. We're the ones who should be treating you."

"Nonsense. The amount of money you saved me by letting me stay here with you is much more than the cost of a couple of meals for the three of us. I've been very lucky on this trip. I've met some great people

68

who insisted I stay with them, so the only hotel expenses I've had were a couple of nights in Yellowstone as well as a night in Billings. I much prefer your spare bedroom to any of the hotel rooms I've stayed in on this trip."

"So how did you manage to find people to stay with?" Jenny inquired.

Jeff took a deep breath. He wondered how he could tell his friends about the people he'd met along the way without telling them of the strange visions he'd been having.

"I was in Sioux Falls and I met someone who actually knew my Uncle David. He took me home to spend the night with them and I met his father who was friends with Grandfather. He was my tour guide while I was in South Dakota and his brother took over from there. It was an education in itself."

"Getting in touch with your Native American heritage?" Karl asked. "It's no wonder you got involved in a pow-wow. I figured your grandfather immersed you in all that stuff."

Jeff sighed deeply. "I wish he had, but he was well aware of my white blood. He tried to give me the best of both worlds without pushing me one way or another. I'm afraid I have a lot to learn. This teaching assignment is going to be a true experience."

In more ways than one, his inner voice cautioned. *The shaman, Alan Turtle, will be able to lead you on the path your life is supposed to take. Just keep an open mind.*

* * * *

On Sunday afternoon, Jeff prepared to leave for his new home, along with his meeting with the elders of the reservation where he would be teaching for the next five years.

"I wish you weren't leaving today," Jenny lamented. "Mom and Aunt Kelly will be here tomorrow and they'll be so sorry they missed you."

"I doubt that. Besides, I'll be seeing them in three weeks at the wedding. That should be enough for them." He knew his answer wasn't the one Jenny wanted to hear, but even though his father's brother and sister came to his grandfather's funeral, he couldn't forget the encounter he'd had with his Grandfather Cooper.

Jenny pretended to pout, but before he finally got into his car for the last leg of his trip, she hugged him tightly. "I'll be looking forward to seeing you again in three weeks," she whispered before giving him a sisterly peck on the cheek.

The warmth of her kiss lingered long after Jeff pulled out onto the highway and started for the place he would soon call home. Had things been different, the two of them might have gotten together as a couple. What a fiasco would that have been? If they'd become involved, sooner or later they would have learned they were kissin' cousins. They weren't related by blood, but with her aunt and his being one in the same the connection would have been too close for anything good to come out of it. It was for the best Jenny and Karl were the ones getting married and he was but a minor player in the scenario.

The warmth of the August morning prompted Jeff to make more stops to enjoy the panorama of scenery playing out before him. The mountains stood in direct contrast to the wooded area of Northern Wisconsin he called home his entire life.

If I live here forever, I'll never get used to this view, Jeff thought as he enjoyed the scenery from the small restaurant where he'd stopped for lunch. After the large breakfast Jenny prepared for him, he'd been certain he could easily skip lunch, but the sign for the roadside café caught his attention and his stomach growled in anticipation.

"What can I get you?" the waitress asked him once he seated himself at the lunch counter.

Jeff looked up from the plastic encased menu into the brown eyes of a young woman with definite Native American ancestry. "What do you suggest?"

"Personally, I like the elk burger, but considering you're not from here, you might prefer the hamburger with the works."

Her comment came as a surprise. "How do you know I'm not from here?"

"It's not rocket science. I saw you pull in with Wisconsin plates on your car. Now, I'll ask you again, what can I get you?"

"Since I'm going to be living here for the next five years, I guess I'll try the elk burger."

The waitress broke into a wide grin. "You must be the new teacher coming to the reservation. I'm Marie Turtle. My grandfather is the shaman. I see him every evening when he comes to my mother's home for dinner. He's been telling me for weeks there's a new teacher coming from Wisconsin. It sounds like we'll be working together."

"I don't understand. How will be we working together?"

"Oh, you mean because I'm working here. My sister and brother-in-law own this place. I've worked here summers ever since I was in high school. During the winter, I teach science in the high school at the reservation. The history teacher retired last year and from what I hear, the elders had problems filling the position."

"I wouldn't know. The name is Jeff Cooper. I'm just glad to have a position to go to. Is there anything I should know about the reservation?"

"Have you ever been on one before?"

"I grew up on the Lac du Flambeau reservation in Wisconsin. My mother was Chippewa and my father was white. They were killed in an accident and my grandfather raised me. He was also a shaman."

"Let me put in your order and then we can talk some more. Things have been pretty slow today. If you don't mind hanging around for a while, I'll lead you out to the reservation. I get off at two."

Jeff smiled at Marie's offer. From the map, he knew the way out to the reservation, but it would be interesting to follow her. He decided she was certainly someone he wanted to get to know.

Within a few minutes, Marie returned with his burger complete with fries and a coke. "I've eaten venison all my life, how close is elk in taste?"

Marie smiled. "I think you're in for a pleasant surprise. Let's just say I know why the people were not impressed with the beef the whites brought them when they were confined to the reservation."

Jeff studied Marie's face. As he did, he remembered the stories his grandfather told about how the tribes were forced onto lands where they couldn't hunt for their families as they had since the beginning of time. Instead, they were forced to accept the handouts from the government that were often contaminated before they ever reached the hands of the people.

"I'll let you know what I think," he replied.

As soon as he took the first bite of his burger, he knew exactly what she was talking about. It didn't carry the gamey taste of the venison he'd grown up eating. It also didn't resemble the beef in the hamburgers he'd come to enjoy while in school. It was much sweeter, and something he knew he would soon come to enjoy during his stay on the reservation where he'd been assigned to teach for the next five years.

"I've never tasted anything like this," he said, once he swallowed the first bite of the sandwich. "I see what you mean. It's a good thing the government finally came to its senses, and allowed the people to not only hunt, but show people how good this natural food is."

"I knew you'd see it our way. So what do you know about the Blackfoot reservation?"

"Not as much as I'd like to know. I stopped in South Dakota and spent some time with Ken and Chuck Hawk. It seems they knew my grandfather and my Uncle David."

"Your grandfather wouldn't be Tom Red Hawk would he?"

Her question took Jeff by surprise. "How did you know?"

"Many years ago, Grandfather went to a conference for shaman in South Dakota. That's where he met Ken and Chuck Hawk as well as your grandfather. They've been in contact ever since. I was sorry to hear of his passing. From what Grandfather tells me, he was a good friend."

Jeff's mind spun. Was it only coincidence he'd been sent to this particular reservation or did his grandfather have a hand in the appointment?

Jeff thoroughly enjoyed talking with Marie until the end of her shift. She told him stories of growing up on the reservation that mirrored his own memories of growing up. As with his home, there was poverty here. It saddened him more than anything else.

Is it possible I could make a difference for the kids I'll be teaching?

What do you think? His grandfather's voice sounded in his head.

Oh, Grandfather. I wish you were here. I need to talk to you.

Alan will help you with everything you've been experiencing. Trust him. He's a good man.

"Are you ready to go?" Marie said, interrupting his silent conversation from the other side.

"Your replacement must have gotten here." He knew it sounded like a stupid question, but it was the first thing to come out of his mouth.

"My brother-in-law got here and my sister will be here as soon as she drops the kids off at Mom's for the evening. I'm free as a bird and more than ready to show you the way to the reservation. I hope you can keep up with me. I've got a hot date with my niece and nephew, and I don't want to be late."

Jeff followed her out to the parking lot. He smiled when she went around to the back of the café and come back out in a beat up pickup truck. It certainly wasn't what he expected to see her driving. He didn't know what he thought she'd be driving but it certainly wasn't a pickup truck.

Chapter Eight

Jeff thought Marie was joking when she taunted him about keeping up with her. Once she turned off the highway onto the gravel road, the only thing he could do was follow the dust left by her vehicle as she sped toward the reservation.

He finally caught up with her as she was getting out of the truck in front of a single story house on a dusty street. If the street had been paved, he would have thought he'd been transported back to his home in Wisconsin.

"I thought you said you could keep up with me," she greeted him.

"I'm not used to driving on gravel roads. I was afraid I might lose control of my car."

"Oh that's right, you're one of those civilized Indians." She was laughing so hard Jeff couldn't be upset with the off-handed verbal slight to him.

"Guess I am. So, is this where you live?"

"This is my mom's place. I live here with her and when I'm done with work, I come and pick up the kiddies and take them out on some kind of an excursion until Mom gets supper ready. They have so much energy, she wouldn't ever get anything for us to eat. I'm sure she'll have plenty for you, if you don't mind eating with us."

Jeff thought for a moment before accepting Marie's generous offer. He'd given no thought to what he would do for meals until he was settled into the housing he'd been assured would be waiting for him upon his arrival.

"I'd appreciate it, especially since I'm sure my accommodations aren't stocked with food. I'll have to do some shopping tomorrow."

"I doubt that," he heard someone say from behind him.

Jeff turned to see an older man with long gray braids coming up the driveway.

"You must be Jeff Copper. I'm Alan Turtle. We don't have separate accommodations for you, but you will be staying with me. I have several extra rooms and usually have some of the teachers living with me until they can find something that suits their needs."

"It's a pleasure to meet you, Sir. I'm told you knew my grandfather as well as my uncle. Ken and Chuck Hawk spoke highly of you as well. I've been looking forward to meeting you."

The older man smiled broadly. "I had a call from Chuck a couple of days ago about you. I think the two of us will be having some interesting discussions. I'm certain it will be like debating with your grandfather. I hope my granddaughter invited you to join us for supper. You'll find we take most of our meals with my daughter. It's not that I can't cook, but she insists I don't eat properly when I'm alone. Maybe with you here, she'll relent and allow us to prepare our own meals. I certainly hope so, since I stocked my cupboards with the good stuff. You do know how to cook, don't you?"

Jeff laughed at the statement. "Grandfather taught me how to cook when I was in high school. I have to admit we had some interesting meals, but we didn't starve, either."

The old man laughed at Jeff's comment. "Why don't we go over to my place and get your gear stored. It will be a good hour and a half before my daughter-in-law has supper ready. It's within walking distance, but we might as well take your car over. That way, between the two of us, we can get your stuff unpacked."

"Don't you go talking the boy's ear off," a woman who looked like an older version of Marie called from the front door. "You know I don't stand for anyone being late for supper."

"When have I ever missed a meal?" Alan asked. "We'll be here in an hour and a half."

Jeff got back into his car and followed Alan's directions to a house that looked much larger than the one where Marie went to corral her niece and nephew.

"I know what you're thinking, why do I have such a big house? When my wife and I first built it, we had a large family. Of course, she passed away several years ago, and the kids have spread to the four winds. Since I have the room, that's why I've been taking in the teachers when they first come here. Most of them are like you and join us for the first five years after their graduation. The ones who stay usually look into their own accommodations."

"I had most of my stuff sent on ahead," Jeff said as he pulled his suitcases from the trunk of the car.

"I know. They arrived last week and were brought here. I've taken the boxes to your room. Of course, you will have the use of the entire house."

Jeff entered the house, and was surprised by the modern accommodations. The living room had a large flat screen television as well as a desk with a laptop computer sitting on it. In the kitchen were older appliances of the finest quality.

"It's not what I expected."

"This house was designed for my wife. Since her passing, I've enjoyed the quality of the appliances she insisted on having put in. I worked in a factory on the other side of the reservation and was the manager of that facility. It wasn't like we couldn't afford the luxury she so enjoyed. It also afforded me with a good pension."

"I don't understand, if you were able to make such a good living, why is there so much poverty?"

"In my day, men were willing to work and reap the benefits of their labors. A lot of us made a good living working at the factory, but then the factory closed, and even though we still had our pensions, there were no jobs for the young men. Then of course, there were the drugs that seemed to take hold of not only our young men and women, but also many of the older generation. We're just now getting back on our feet. There are a lot of small businesses that are taking hold in the area, and giving the kids you will be teaching jobs, if they don't choose to go on to school."

Jeff nodded. He knew the devastation brought about by the drug trade. He'd seen it firsthand both at home and in Madison while he'd been at the University.

"I'm told you're going to be teaching history," Alan continued. "Will you be teaching only the history of the white men?"

"That was the plan, but things have changed since I arrived in South Dakota."

"Ah yes, the visions you've been having. Chuck and Ken both talked to me about what you've been experiencing, Blue Eagle Feather."

Alan's use of the name Ken insisted should be his *man* name came as a surprise. He'd heard about vision quests and questioned how anything like that could happen to a young man. Having seen the eagle and receiving the blue eagle feather, he now had more questions than answers about what path his life was going to take.

"Chuck and Ken both told me you'd be able to explain these visions to me."

"All in due time, Jeff, all in due time. For now, we'd better get over to Donna's for supper or she'll have my scalp hanging from her doorpost. You heard her; no one is late for meals at her table."

Jeff agreed. Even though he'd stopped for lunch and eaten more than he'd planned, he felt the pains of hunger gnawing at his stomach. Without unpacking anything, he left his suitcases in the room Alan assigned to him. As soon as he entered the bedroom, he saw the boxes he'd packed before leaving Wisconsin and sent on ahead by UPS.

Even though he knew Marie and her mother expected them there for supper, he took a moment to look around the room. Although Alan's home was larger and more modern than the one he shared with his grandfather, Jeff was immediately reminded of home. The large bedroom looked out on the mountains, but if he closed his eyes, the smell of sage was the aroma of home.

He took a moment to sit down on the bed and think about his grandfather. *Why didn't I listen more closely when you talked about your life as a shaman?*

Because you were young and hungry for the education you received at the University, and I wanted to spare you the life I've led. Do not get me wrong. I have had a good life, but it has also been a burden I wanted to save you from.

His grandfather's words within his mind were more confusing the comforting. *Am I a shaman, Grandfather? Are the visions I've been having only the beginning?*

Chapter Nine

Jeff's life soon fell into a comfortable routine. Each evening, he took his meals at Donna's home, and always looked forward to seeing Marie as well as the children sharing the table with him. While Jeff prepared their breakfast each day, Alan insisted on taking on the responsibility of making lunch. Jeff looked forward to Alan's lunches, as they often included a hamper filled with sandwiches as they explored the remote corners of the reservation.

"Once you start school, these excursions will have to come to an end," Alan said as they drove to yet another unexplored area of the reservation.

"I'm going to miss them, but we always have the weekends. I have to admit, I'm looking forward to getting into the classroom. I'm anxious to meet the kids, and have been revising my study guides. I thought maybe we could talk about it today."

Alan smiled. "I'd like that. What are you thinking about?"

"As you know, I have to teach US history the way it's portrayed in the history books, but I'm thinking about giving a midterm project of writing a term paper on Native American culture. For reference, I'm going to ask the kids to use the information at the cultural center along with stories from their parents and grandparents. Of course, before we start on the project, we will have a three week study of our culture."

"I agree, but how do you propose to do the three week study?"

"That's where I need your help. I would like to have you and some of the other elders come in to lead the lectures. As you know, I have a college education, but you have a lifetime of education. Somehow I get the impression that like me, the young people of this reservation know a little bit about their culture, but they don't know about the heart of the people."

Alan was silent for a moment, then nodded his approval. "I like that. The heart of the people. I know several elders who would be interested in this project of yours. Give me a few days, and I'm sure I can put together a meeting of elders, not only from this reservation, but also from several others around the country. This could be something great."

Jeff was pleased with Alan's acceptance of his idea. It would be something unheard of to get together the leaders from several tribes to talk about the history of the people.

Thinking about his exciting project, propelled Jeff into an unexpected vision. Within it, the grassy plain where they were eating lunch turned into a village from the past. Men were returning from the hunt, and women were rejoicing at the bounty of the harvested food for their survival. Children ran toward the returning hunters, many of whom were teenagers who had just completed their vision quests and were riding with the adult hunters for the first time.

Drums beat and singers sang the praises of the men who brought food to their fires. As they did, Jeff recognized one of the older drummers as a previous incarnation of himself. He felt the beat of the drums deep in his soul and was surprised when he recognized the words of praise coming from the singers.

Even though he wanted to remain lost in the vision, it faded from his view, and he was once again alone with Alan getting ready to share the lunch they'd packed earlier in the day.

"Your vision was very vivid," Alan commented. "I agree with Chuck. To watch you engrossed in a vision is something I never thought I would see. My father used to tell of the shaman of old who would become lost in their visions, and what a miracle it was to watch. You are destined to become a great man among our people. Are you certain your grandfather never trained you to follow in his footsteps?"

"I'm sure. Being half-white, I'm positive he never thought I had the capabilities to become a shaman. In his mind it was better if I trained to teach the young, and hopefully carry on the traditions of the past."

"I doubt that. I just don't think the time you had with him was the right time. From what Ken and Chuck told me, your native spirit was not awakened until you arrived at the sacred falls of the Sioux."

"You're right. I lived all my life on the reservation back home, and have never had the experiences I've had in the past month. As much as I want to be a teacher and devote my life to the kids, I have to acknowledge what has been happening in my life."

"That's what I wanted to hear you say. I know you will be leaving tomorrow for your friend's wedding. By the time you return, I will have contacted the elders. Then we have a week to come up with a program for your classroom before you start the new school year. I will tell you, it won't be easy. These kids are more interested in sex, drugs and booze than they are in going to school. With many of their families dependent on the government, they know they have to go to school and work for little more than mercy 'D's' to pass their classes so they can eventually graduate. It is the future that is at stake for these young people. Between you, me and the elders, maybe we can make some monumental changes in their lives."

Chapter Ten

Jeff pulled up in front of Karl and Jenny's apartment. Although only less than a hundred miles separated the modern city from the reservation Jeff now called home, he knew much more than the mileage separated them. The people he now called his neighbors and would soon consider friends, were not the same college educated friends. Jenny was already working as a nurse in an ultra-modern hospital, while Karl was engrossed in his internship at the same facility. He doubted either one of them would fit into his new life.

"I didn't think you'd ever get here, Buddy," Karl said as he came out to greet him. "All of the other groomsmen are here and looking forward to going out golfing. The girls are all out doing whatever it is girls do, so we were just waiting for you to get here."

As soon as Jeff stowed his gear, he was no longer the half-breed on the reservation preparing to teach history, and dealing with unwanted visions that were sending his life in a completely different direction. Here he was with his friends from college, the guys he'd grown up with, from gangly teenagers to men, ready to tackle whatever road life took them on.

"It's about time you got here Coop," Pete Armstrong greeted him.

He'd forgotten the nickname he'd been given by these friends in college. It has been only three months since anyone called him Coop, and yet it felt as though a lifetime had passed.

"I've been getting settled on the reservation. After the wedding, I'll be going back to work with the elders in setting up my teaching schedule for the next year."

"What's there to set up?" Pete asked. "I'm teaching in Omaha and I just have to follow the program that's in place."

Jeff laughed at his friend's statement. "Things are different here than they are in the big city. I've got a bunch of kids who think they can slough off and pass their classes with a 'D' because they have no prospects on the reservation. I hope I can change all of that."

"You always were reaching for the pie in the sky. Well, for this weekend, we're here to have fun, and there will be no work talk," Karl declared.

It didn't take long for Jeff to stow his duffel bag and get ready to go golfing. For this weekend, the apartment Karl shared with Jenny became Bachelor Center, while Jenny and her girlfriends were being pampered at a bed and breakfast on the other side of town.

Although Jeff tried to turn off his mind and concentrate on his friends, he continued to mull over the new curriculum he would be presenting to the elders when he returned to the reservation.

After they finished their golf outing, they went out for the evening to a local strip club. Even though his friends enjoyed hooting and hollering at the dancers and shoving dollar bills into their G-strings, Jeff remained more subdued than he'd ever been at one of these outings when they'd been in college. Back then, he'd been a carefree young man. Now he had a heavier weight on his shoulders than he could ever share with his friends.

* * * *

Friday night, Jeff and his friends gathered at the church where the wedding would be held the next day. It was the first time he would be coming face to face with his Aunt Kelly. Seeing her now, without the stress of their first meeting, he was able to see the likeness of his father in her eyes. Granted he was only a young boy when his parents were killed, but every night he'd studied their pictures and they were one of the first things he put up in the room he would be using in Alan's home.

"It's good to see you again, Jeff," Kelly said as she came up to give him a hug.

As much as he wanted to hold her at arm's length, she represented the family from his father's side he longed for all his life.

I know I should reject this part of my family, and yet they offer something I've been missing.

Do not think you dishonor your heritage by getting to know your father's sister. She is a good woman and only wants to have a part in your life.

Hearing his grandfather's voice within the confines of his mind should have come as a surprise, but nothing shocked him any longer. Instead, it was a comfort to know he could embrace the white side of his family, and still be free to discover what his life as Blue Eagle Feather would entail.

"I was sorry we missed you when we first came out to help with the wedding," Kelly said.

Jeff hoped she hadn't made any other statements he should remember while he'd been listening to his grandfather's logic within the confines of his mind.

"I knew I'd be seeing you this weekend, and I had to get to the reservation so I could get settled."

"I wanted to ask you about that. Are you finally settled? Were you able to find an apartment?"

"The answers are yes and no. I'm staying with Alan Turtle. He's one of the elders and the local shaman. Since he has a large home, he takes in teachers to give them a place to stay until they decide if they want to continue on after the first five years. We make a good team. His daughter-in-law cooks dinner for us each evening, but for breakfast and lunch, we're on our own. I'm glad I listened to my grandfather when he insisted I learn how to cook."

"It sounds like you have an ideal situation. Here I was thinking you were probably going to be wasting away to nothingness by having to do your own cooking."

Jeff laughed at Kelly's statement. "Even if I'd had my own apartment, you wouldn't have to worry. I wouldn't have starved. As it is, I'm eating some of the best food I've had in a long time. We all know how college students eat. To be honest, if I never saw another pizza it would be too soon for me."

Their conversation was interrupted when the minister called everyone in the wedding to the front of the church to give them their final instructions. As best man, it was Jeff's responsibility to be in charge of the wedding ring Karl would be giving Jenny during the ceremony the next day.

Once they were finished at the church, everyone went over to Karl's parent's home to enjoy the rehearsal dinner. While everyone had been at the church, the neighbors of the River's family worked at putting together a great bar-b-que complete with a steer they'd been cooking all day.

After filling his plate, Jeff found a table with his friends, minus Karl, who made it quite clear he wanted to be alone with Jenny. They'd agreed to separate at midnight so they wouldn't see each other until on the day of the wedding.

As he enjoyed the easy banter of his friends, his mind wandered to the life he would be living as Blue Eagle Feather. He thought about the lovely science teacher, Marie Turtle. She told him she'd graduated high school at the age of seventeen, and worked harder than most to complete her four-year degree in three years. The fact she'd been teaching for two years made her no more than a year older than him. Once he returned to the reservation, would he be able to court her and bridge the gap in their ages? He certainly hoped so.

By the end of the evening, he sought out Kelly. "I know you were on the reservation in Wisconsin when you came to Grandfather's funeral, but I would like to show you where I'll be living and working for the next five years."

"Do you think we'd be welcome?" Kelly asked.

"I don't see why not. You are part of my family, the white part. They know I'm a half breed. If you'd feel better about it, I'd be happy to give Alan a call and see what he thinks."

"I'd really like to, but unfortunately, I've taken all of my vacation time to come out and help my sister-in-law with the wedding. I have to be back at work on Monday morning, so we'll be flying back to Chicago after the kids open their presents on Sunday afternoon."

Jeff was disappointed, but he understood. "I can give you a rain check and an open invitation."

"I'd like that. We're planning to come out next summer and do some sightseeing. If you plan to spend your summer on the reservation, we'd enjoy taking you up on your invitation."

85

* * * *

The wedding, like all weddings was an elaborate affair. Jenny was every inch the beautiful bride, who could have just stepped off the cover of one of the Bridal magazines Jeff saw in their apartment when he stayed with them on his way to the reservation.

At the reception, he'd danced with several of Jenny's friends, including some of her sorority sisters from college. They were all girls he'd known and socialized with while in school, and he enjoyed seeing them again.

On Sunday, they all gathered at Karl's parents' home for a light lunch while the happy couple opened presents. As gift after gift was opened, Jeff wondered how his friends would feel about his present. He'd given it a lot of thought, and along with a gift card he'd picked up at the local mall. In addition, he bought them a bottle of wine at a local winery, and as a last minute addition, picked up a dream catcher from one of the craftswomen at the reservation.

Finally, Jenny chose the gift bag standing among the beautifully wrapped presents. As soon as she pulled out the bottle of wine, he realized he'd been holding his breath in anticipation of his friends opening his gift.

"Oh, this is just perfect Jeff," she declared. Reaching further into the bag, she pulled out first the gift card, and then the dream catcher the craftswoman insisted on wrapping separately. As soon as they opened the small package, the other people present began to ooh and aah over the spider web weave of the dream catcher. Within the weave, small beads along with feathers had been added to insure the sweet dreams of the newly married couple.

"What a fantastic gift," Kelly said.

He hadn't even seen her come to his side. "Coming from me, I thought it was appropriate."

"I've always been intrigued by those things. Do they really insure sweet dreams?"

"That's what the woman who made it assured me when I bought it. I know I always had one over my bed when I was a kid, and I don't ever remember having nightmares."

His statement brought a laugh before his aunt returned her attention to the other gifts being opened by Jenny and Karl.

Instead of concentrating on the presents, he allowed his mind to focus on dreams. Maybe his dream catcher had kept away the nightmares, but there was nothing he could do about the visions that plagued him ever since he entered South Dakota, and received the name of Blue Eagle Feather.

Chapter Eleven

On his way back to the reservation, Jeff went to the airport to say good-bye to his aunt and uncle before they checked in for their flight. With the obligatory farewell said, he turned his car towards the place he now called home.

Driving past the diner where he'd stopped on the day he first came here, he automatically looked for Marie's truck. Even though he knew the diner closed at two on Sunday, he was disappointed to see the empty parking lot. In the twilight of early evening, he understood he was too late for supper at Donna's house, he hoped he'd be able to stop to see Marie.

As he drove past Donna's home, he was disappointed not to see Marie's vehicle. He was about to turn the corner, when he saw her in the backyard. After making a quick U-turn, he pulled up in front and parked. If Marie was still there, perhaps Alan would be there as well, and he could give the old man a ride home.

"When did you get back?" Marie greeted him.

"I just pulled into town."

"So how was the wedding?" Donna asked. "Did your friends like their gift?"

Jeff described the reception his gift received and remembered it was Donna who suggested where to find something special for his friends.

"So," Alan began, "are you ready to get to work tomorrow?"

Jeff took a deep breath. "As ready as I'll ever be. I did a lot of thinking this weekend and decided I would spend the first couple of weeks outlining the history of America, and then get into the real point of why I'm here."

Alan smiled. "The elders and I have been talking about this while you were gone. We all agree with the course of study you're planning. I think you'll be excited about what they will be presenting to you this coming week."

* * * *

Jeff felt his meeting with the elders was very productive. He now had pages and pages of notes to look over before coming to any concrete decisions about what he would be teaching for the coming year.

The stories he heard from the older men were not only those of the Plaines Indians, but also history of the tribes in the East who had first encountered the men with white skin. These were not the same as the stories he'd learned from reading historical fiction or watching the many movies put out about the disputes between whites, and the first inhabitants of the land now known as the United States.

He knew of the diseases brought by the white man, but what he didn't know were the traditions observed by any of the people who stood in their way as they claimed the lands from sea to shining sea.

He now surveyed his classroom. Rather than the usual map of the United States, he'd searched the Internet until he found one depicting where the various tribes lived prior to the white invasion. When he dug further into the information, he learned he could buy copies of the map from a small bookstore in Casper. Once he told them how he planned to use the map, they suggested not only the large copy to hang in the front of his classroom, but also a smaller version he could use to make copies for his students.

The first day of school, he was so nervous he could only drink a cup of coffee because of the flock of butterflies that had taken up residence in his stomach. He'd done practice teaching in Wisconsin, but those students weren't his sole responsibility. He'd merely been there to learn rather than to teach.

Even though Alan protested Jeff's decision to skip breakfast, he said he understood the case of nerves that were plaguing him.

The map he'd hung the day before brought a smile to his lips. Beside it, on the board, he wrote MR. JEFF COOPER – BLUE EAGLE FEATHER. It felt good to link both his white name and the one given to him by his Spirit Guide.

As his students entered the room, he realized just what a challenge teaching at this school would be. Even though Marie warned him about the kids who would be in his class, he was taken aback.

Many of the boys had long hair, but rather than in the braids of their heritage, they wore them as dread locks. Their jeans were ripped, and the shirts they wore had seen better days. Although he knew the area was in poverty, he realized these kids were making a statement against the establishment.

The next thing he noticed were the ear buds worn by many of the kids. He knew they ran to the IPods, phones, or tablets hiding in their book bags.

"Good morning," he greeted them when the final bell rang. "I'm the new guy here. As you can see, my name is on the board."

"Hey man, are you shittin' us with that Indian name along with your white one?" One of the young men sitting about mid room asked.

"Six months ago I would have asked the same question. Then I started my trip to come here and experienced a vision in which my Spirit Guide gave me my 'man' name."

"Do you believe in all that vision quest shit?" another teenager asked.

"I do now. I also want to lay a few grounds rules for this class. I don't expect you to cut your hair, but I'm sure your families would prefer a more traditional look. Also, I'm sure your parents would like you to look presentable rather than wearing ripped jeans and dirty shirts. That said, this is going to be a different kind of history class than any you've been in before. I came here to teach American History, but I'm sure you know the entire white version of the story. This year, we are going to be studying 'our' heritage. The story of the people who claimed this country for their own, long before the whites came here. As you can see, the map behind us shows where each of the tribes lived before the states, as we know them were formed. Last but not least, I won't stand for any more of the profanity I heard when you first entered the class room. I know you've all been taught how to speak in front of each other as well as your elders, and I expect you to abide by the rules your parents set for you."

"Are you really Native American?" A petite girl at the back of the classroom asked.

"Like many of you I have white blood, but I grew up with my grandfather who was a shaman on the Lac du Flambeau reservation in Northern Wisconsin. My father was white, therefore I have the last name of Cooper. When I was your age, I didn't want anything to do with the Chippewa heritage, but I didn't have much choice because my parents were killed in a car accident when I was very young. I wanted an education, but I knew my grandfather couldn't afford to give it to me. That's when I found out I could get a scholarship to the University of Wisconsin in Madison in exchange for teaching for five years on a reservation."

"So, man, you're only here because you have to be in order to not have to pay for your college education. What a line of crap. Of course, what else can you expect from a do-gooder half breed? I can just hear what you'll be telling all your college friends about the poor little Indian kids you've been teaching."

"I hope to change your mind about me by the end of the term. I have to tell you, I was going to teach the same old course until I got here, and met the elders as well as the people in your village. You'll learn more about me, little by little, but today I want to get to know you."

One by one, the kids got to their feet and gave their names as well as a little information about themselves.

The final bell rang and the first students got to their feet to leave, when Jeff stopped them. "Tomorrow we'll begin our work. Today, we got to know each other, but tomorrow we will assign seats and start to gain respect for one another. The first step will be knowing I will not tolerate electronic devices in the classroom, so please leave your IPods, phones, and tablets in your lockers."

There were many murmurs, perhaps even grumblings until the young man with the dreads spoke up. "Mr. C is right. I think his class is going to be entirely different from any we've been to before."

The others ceased their grumbling, and continued on out into the hall. Only the boy who spoke up turned back. "I think you'll see an entirely different class tomorrow, including me."

Throughout the day, Jeff found his other classes were more subdued and receptive to the things he told them in the introduction to their being in his class. He couldn't help but wonder if the belligerent young man from his first class, Jason Wild Horse, had told the other students about his unorthodox program of study.

"I'm hearing a lot of good things about the new teacher in our midst," Marie said when they met in the teacher's lounge after the last class of the day. "It seems like you made quite an impression on Jason."

"I wondered if he had anything to do with it," he commented. "I couldn't believe the difference between the first hour class and the rest of my classes throughout the day."

"Jason is popular with the other kids, but every teacher in this school has had a run in with him at one time or another. It started when he decided to wear his hair in dreads and adopt his current wardrobe. His mother and mine are good friends, and she's also at the end of her rope with him. She's afraid he'll be getting into the drugs that are so common on the reservation. His father was killed in a car accident while he was driving drunk. It's a real problem here. I hope you're able to get through to him this year."

Jeff shook his head. Maybe he'd hit a nerve with Jason, but he doubted if he would make any difference in the young man's life. Surely, these kids knew the history of their people, but between Alan, the elders and his own visions, he felt the need to reinforce the history these young people needed to hear and embrace.

* * * *

"How was your first day?" Donna asked at dinner that evening.

Jeff hesitated before answering. Surely, she'd heard about what went on at the school from Marie. "It was enlightening to say the very least. I met a very interesting student. His name is Jason Wild Horse. Marie tells me you and his mother are good friends."

Donna nodded. "That is true. I know Judy has been very worried about her son. He's been defiant ever since his father was killed. I hope and pray you will be a good influence on him."

"I would like that too, but you have to remember, I'm the outsider here. I don't even know how to interpret my visions."

"Don't worry about your visions, Jeff," Alan said, joining the conversation for the first time. "When the time is right, your Spirit Guide will allow me to interpret them for you. I think the way you're proposing to do your classes is part of the reason your Spirit Guide has taken this time to communicate with you. In time, all will be revealed."

Jeff tried to be patient, but even though he was now considered an adult, he realized he wanted things to go quickly and be revealed immediately. He was the first to admit, patience wasn't his strong point in life.

* * * *

Jeff took extra care in dressing for his second day of class at his new school. Instead of the suit and tie he'd worn for the first day, he opted for a western shirt and blue jeans along with the moccasins he purchased from the same craftswoman who sold him the dream catcher for Karl and Jenny.

"You look good in the less formal mode of dress," Alan said. "It's exactly what they need to turn them around. It will be interesting to see how they interact with you."

Jeff reviewed the conversation he'd engaged in with Alan as he stepped into his classroom. From out of nowhere, another vision took over his conscious thought. In front of his eyes, the room with its desks in neat rows transformed to a village with a large fire in the center of a sacred circle. In the vision, the elders of the village talked to the young men and women and told them the stories of their people from the past.

Before his eyes, his Spirit Guide materialized and seated itself on the desk closest to where Jeff stood. *You are here to reveal the past to your students, but not in this setting. Bring them back to their heritage, and show them how things were in the past. Teach them in the way of the ancients. American history begins with the people who came before the white men.*

With the same speed as the vision appeared, the reality of present time filled Jeff's mind. He started arranging the desks in a semi-circle in front of the windows facing the mountains. Lastly, he placed his desk so his back would be to the mountains while he could face the students.

"Do you need some help, Mr. C?" He heard someone ask from the direction of the door leading to the hallway.

Without looking up, he knew the voice belonged to Jason, and gladly accepted his student's help. When Jason entered his line of vision, he was more than surprised. If he'd met the kid in the hallway, he wouldn't have equated him with the young man standing in front of him.

Rather than the dread locks of one day earlier, his tight dreads had been taken down, and his hair washed and brushed until it shone. Replacing the dreads were two neat braids trailing over his shoulders. His ripped jeans were replaced with ones that still looked as though they'd just come from the store, and he wore a plaid shirt neatly tucked into his pants. Rather than moccasins like the ones Jeff wore, he had on a pair of boots. It was evident they weren't new, and Jeff assumed they might have been ones his father had worn.

"Did I surprise you?" Jason asked.

Jeff ran his fingers through his hair. "I should have expected it. You did say I'd see you in a different light this morning. Can I expect the same from your classmates?"

"I hope so. We all had a meeting yesterday at lunch and thought it was only right to give you a chance to show us your teaching method. We're hoping it will be different. I like the way you've arranged the room."

Jason quickly took one side of the desk and helped Jeff to move it to the position in front of the windows.

"It's a shame you'll be missing this view, but aren't you afraid we'll all be distracted by it?"

"I'm hoping it will inspire you to learn more of the heritage of 'our' people."

More and more students began to enter the room, and as Jason predicted, Jeff saw the difference in his students immediately, if not in appearance, in attitude. Once the seats were assigned, Jason came up to where Jeff was standing.

"Before we start," Jason said, taking command of his fellow students. "Like we said yesterday, Mr. C. seems like an upright guy. As you can see, I'm ready to make a change, and I hope the rest of you are with me."

There were several murmurs among the students while Jason took his seat. "I appreciate your vote of confidence, Jason. I'm also sure you are wondering about the configuration of this room. Before the coming of the white man to these lands, the villages were set up in a semi-circle with the opening of the lodges facing to the east. I realize your desks are facing to the west, but this was the closest I could come. Also, when the ancients wanted to tell the younger generation the stories of the past, they stood in the middle of the sacred circle. I would rather have you in a semi-circle so I do not have my back to any of you. Since the first contact the whites had, were with the tribes of the East, I've decided that's where we will start."

"What about the Mandan?" Jason asked. "I read a book about the Welch who came to this country long before the pilgrims ever landed at Plymouth Rock."

Jeff knew what book he was talking about, but it surprised him to have Jason mention it. He'd found it in the library at the university, but when he wanted to buy a copy of it, he had to search long and hard on the internet to find one. "I read the same book. Unfortunately, disease killed off the Mandan before anyone could ever prove they had Welch blood. It's a great theory, but it's only a theory."

By the end of the class period, several other students joined in the discussion, and Jeff could tell this was going to be a productive year.

Chapter Twelve

Although Jason transformed himself on the second day of school, it took the other students longer to adapt to a more acceptable dress code, and grooming practices. By Thanksgiving, they'd talked about the history of the Native American tribes intermingled with the arrival of the whites, and the numerous wars fought for the independence of this great nation. The study of the French and Indian wars, as well as the life of Tecumapese, were especially well received by the students. The last white history they touched on prior to the Thanksgiving break had been the War of 1812. Jeff could tell his students were not as interested in the white history, but he would be remiss if he didn't teach the basics along with the history the kids were interested in learning.

"Tomorrow begins the Thanksgiving break," he announced on the last morning of class. "I know we've progressed past the first Thanksgiving, but what do you think about the circumstances surrounding that historic day?"

Ellen Colt raised her hand. "I think the people saw the whites as neighbors who were having a hard time surviving in 'their' world. They were being neighborly without knowing what was coming and how these intruders would change their lives."

"Good point," Jeff commented. "In the beginning of the whites coming to North America, the people were more accepting of their strange looking neighbors. In the past, they'd fought with other tribes, but their enemies always resembled themselves. I'm sure they didn't know how to accept these new people coming to their shores. What it was that broke down relations between the tribes and the newcomers, we will probably never know. Just like the lost colony at Jamestown, it will remain a mystery in this great nation."

Philip Wolf was the next to raise his hand. "Was there ever a time when the US military and the Native Americans worked together?"

Jeff smiled, encouraged by the questions being posed by his students. "By the time we get to WWII, we will be hearing about the Navaho Code Talkers. I've been able to get a DVD of the movie and we'll be watching it sometime next spring. Before that, we need to look into the Civil War as well as the Indian wars. It's taken us a long time to gain the respect of the whites, so that is why it's so important for your generation to change things through education. I think each one of you can relate to what drugs and alcohol are doing to 'our' people. Hopefully, for this reservation, this plague will end with you."

He glanced at Jason, and could see what he said was having a great impact on the young man.

"How can things change when there are no jobs?"

"Believe me, Jason, the elders are working on it. As you know, there are a lot of craftsmen and women in our community. They are also looking into reopening the manufacturing plant. I know this all takes time, but they are interested in knowing what the young people think they could do to bring prosperity back to this area. That's your assignment for the Thanksgiving break. I know a lot of you will be going hunting, but while you're out in the woods, think about what might be a new direction for your community to be taking."

"But we're just kids," Janet Elkhorn protested. "Who's going to listen to us?"

"I promise you, the elders will. I've been working with them, and they are planning a seminar to be held for not only the adults, but also the teenagers of this community for Christmas break. From what I hear, it will be a three day long conference, and there will be guest speakers from several of the other tribes, including my Uncle David from Wisconsin and the Hawk family from South Dakota."

The class was dismissed, as were all the classes that day with the assignment to think about what they wanted to happen within their community in the future.

By the time Jeff returned home, he was more than ready to pack up his car and leave for Karl and Jenny's place for Thanksgiving. He'd been torn about his decision, but his friends said they needed him to come and join them. At the same time, Marie and her family asked him to join them. After weighing up both options, he decided getting away for even a few days would be good for him. His visions were coming at the most inopportune times, leaving him with far more questions than answers.

"I think you need to get away for a few days," Marie said as she helped him pack his car. "I'm sure your friends are looking forward to having you visit them."

"I wish you'd change your mind and come with me."

"My place is here. It doesn't mean I don't care for you, because I do, but being apart won't be such a terrible thing. Grandfather has asked me to work with him and the council of elders in setting up the conference. With school, this is the only time I'll have to work with them."

Jeff knew she was right. From the first time he'd met her, he wanted her in his life. He also knew he had to prove himself, not only to her, but also to the other people of the community he called home. Then there was the meaning of the visions he'd been experiencing for the past five months.

He'd just taken Marie in his arms and kissed her good-bye when his cell phone rang. Thinking it was probably Karl asking when he was leaving, he didn't check the caller ID before answering.

"Hello, Buddy," he greeted his caller.

"J-Jeff," the woman on the other end of the line said. "Th-this is your Aunt Kelly. I'm just calling to tell you my father, your grandfather, died last night. C-can you come to Rockford for the funeral on Saturday?"

Her request caught him completely off guard. The thought of going to mourn the death of the man who wanted nothing to do with him seemed to be hypocritical. On the other hand, he knew his aunt was hurting, and it was possible he could give her some sort of comfort.

"Are you sure he would want me there?"

"It doesn't matter what he wants. It's what I want as well as what my brother, Paul, wants. Our family has been fractured for far too long because of our father. We need to put the pieces back together, and hopefully his funeral will be the beginning of a new relationship for all of us."

Jeff took a deep breath before answering. "I'm just getting ready to leave to spend Thanksgiving with Karl and Jenny. I'll give you a call from their place once I arrive."

"I can understand your need to think about this, but if it's the money for the ticket that's standing in your way, Paul and I are more than willing to send you tickets for a flight on Friday afternoon. I've checked the schedule and…"

"I don't want you to get your hopes up, Aunt Kelly. I'll think about it and call you tomorrow morning. For now, I need to get on the road before it gets too much later."

He ended the call and turned back to Marie. He could see the concern in her eyes.

"Something is terribly wrong, isn't it?"

Jeff nodded. He didn't need to tell her the story of the white side of his family. They'd discussed it several times since his arrival. "My paternal grandfather has passed away. My aunt and uncle want me to come to Rockford for the funeral on Saturday. I'm not sure what I should do."

Marie thought for a moment. "I see no decision to be made here. Even if your grandfather wanted nothing to do with you, it's evident your aunt and uncle want you in their lives. Do not think about it as going there for him, but for them."

"Where are you talking about going?" Alan asked as he joined them.

Once again, Jeff repeated the reason for the phone call from Illinois. "I know Aunt Kelly and Uncle Paul want me there, but I can't put aside the hurt that old man caused me as well as my father over the years."

"I understand what you are saying," Alan agreed. "Since you told your aunt you wouldn't be calling her back until tomorrow, take this night to make your decision. I suggest you pray both to the God of your father and your Spirit Guide. Between the two of them, they will give you the answer you require. Whichever path you choose, it will be the one that is right for you. I will see you Sunday night when you return to this village. May God and the Great Spirit guide you, and bring you safely back to us."

Rather than getting into his car, Jeff returned to his room and came back with the suit, dress shirt, tie, and dress shoes he hadn't worn since the first day of school.

"Have you decided to join your family to pay your respects?" Marie asked when he came back to put his dress clothes in the car.

"Not really, but if I do decide to go, I don't what to show up looking like the poor relations. I owe it to Aunt Kelly and Uncle Paul to dress respectfully."

Marie hugged him tightly and whispered in his ear. "I know you'll make the right decision. Just let us know what you're planning to do."

With a promise to keep in contact, Jeff finally pulled out onto the highway and headed toward Karl and Jenny's apartment. Throughout the trip, he prayed for the wisdom to make the right decision about what to do over the next few days. His plans to kick back and relax with his friends were now up in the air. He needed the down time, and yet there were people in Illinois who needed him to be with them as well.

"Are you going back to Illinois?" Jenny asked once he brought his bags up to their apartment.

"How did you know?" he inquired, completely bewildered by her question.

"Aunt Kelly called me after she talked to you."

"Did she ask you to convince me to come to the funeral on Saturday?"

"Not really. Even if she had, I would have told her the decision has to be yours."

"Thank you," he said with a sigh of relief. "I've been contemplating my answer all the way here. Maybe if I sleep on it, I'll have an answer to give her tomorrow morning."

"Good, for tonight let's go out and get something to eat and maybe have a couple of drinks," Karl suggested. "Jenny has agreed to be our designated driver so if you want to get blotto, we'll get home safely."

For the first time since leaving for the weekend, Jeff smiled. "Getting blotto might not take too long. I haven't had anything to drink other than water, coffee and tea since your wedding. It's just not done on the reservation, at least not by the people I stay with or by me. You know what they say about Indians and firewater. Besides, it's such a problem on the reservation, I didn't want to become part of the epidemic."

"I gathered as much from our conversations these past few months,"

Karl said. "You mentioned how alcohol is a problem. What about hard drugs?"

Jeff shook his head in dismay. "I'd be a liar if I said they weren't a problem. I've got some great kids in my classes, but I'm not blind to the problem. One of my best students, Jason, has a lot of demons. His dad was killed while driving drunk. When I got there the kid had a real attitude problem. He dressed like he didn't care and wore his hair in dreads. I told everyone in the class I wouldn't tolerate my students being slobs. I was surprised the next morning to see him wearing his hair in traditional braids and appropriate clothing. It took some of the other students longer to come around, but they're cleaning up their act so to say."

"Enough shop talk," Jenny declared. "Karl promised me a night out, and I don't want to waste it with shop talk. I have made reservations for us at the Old Miner's Dining Club, so let's get going."

On the way out to eat, Karl explained Jenny's choice of restaurant. "I've been working nights ever since the wedding. To say I was lucky to get this weekend off would be an understatement. I've been promising to take her some place nice for having to put up with my crazy hours. She says the nurses can't quit raving about this place, so tonight we'll see if all the hype is correct."

Jeff was surprised when they pulled up to the restaurant. It wasn't what he'd expected. From the outside, he expected to see delicate furnishings, instead he was immediately entranced by the Native American paintings along with the artifacts around the interior of the restaurant.

"I hope the two of you are hungry," Jenny said as she perused the menu. "These portions are absolutely humungous."

Jeff looked at the menu to see what she meant. The size of the steaks listed were definitely man sized portions. Considering they came with sides as well as desserts made the price a good value for the money.

While Jenny ordered the grilled salmon with the strawberry spinach salad with corn on the cob and breadsticks, she also ordered the cheesecake for dessert.

Although the salmon didn't appeal to them, the guys each opted for the T-Bone steaks with mushrooms and corn on the cob along with brownies with ice cream for dessert.

"How are we ever going to be hungry for Thanksgiving dinner tomorrow?" Jeff asked. "If I eat all of this, I won't be hungry for a week."

"I doubt that," Karl teased. "I remember some of those all you can eat buffets we went to while we were in school. You said the same thing every time we headed back to the dorm. Of course, the next morning, you were the first one at the breakfast table. I doubt you'll have any problem with Mom's dinner at three tomorrow afternoon."

Jeff admitted he hadn't binged on food in a long time, and was looking forward to the entre he'd just ordered. While they waited for their food to be served, he fixated on the painting of the teepees on the open prairie hanging on the wall opposite his chair.

It didn't take long for his vision to take him within the painting. In his vision, he entered the teepee closest to him. Inside he saw the neatly stacked blankets and a welcoming fire pit that gave off a warmth against the chill of the November night they'd just left.

At one time, you lived this life. It is your destiny to save the heritage of those you teach. Remember everything you see here. This is the key to the future as well as to the past.

"Jeff, are you all right?"

The sound of Karl's concerned voice dissolved the vision Jeff became lost in. "Oh, yes, sure. I'm just fine. I was intrigued with this painting." He pointed to the one that inspired his vision. "I know the ancestors lived in these lodges, but I honestly don't know how they stayed warm in the winter."

"If I didn't know better, I would have thought you were somewhere other than here," Jenny said. "You had a faraway look in your eyes as though you were actually one with the painting."

Jeff took a deep breath. His friends were coming dangerously close to the truth surrounding his visions, and until he understood what they meant, he was reluctant to confirm their assumptions.

"Maybe I was," he admitted. "You know it was a long drive to get here, and since school let out at noon today, I skipped lunch in order to get on the road early."

Before Karl or Jenny could comment further, their entrees were served and all talk about visions or hunger was pushed to the side. After taking the first taste of their meal, they became engrossed in eating the delicious food on their plates.

By the time dessert was served, they were each so full they wondered how they could eat another morsel, but somehow managed to make the delicious desserts disappear with very little effort.

"Was everything satisfactory?" their host, Jim Sobonya asked once they were finished.

"More than satisfactory," Karl said. "It's been a long time since I've had a meal like this. I'm a resident at the hospital, and meals for me are catch as catch can. My friend has been living up on the reservation, and something tells me he hasn't been eating steaks like the one we had tonight."

Jeff nodded although in his mind he was thinking about the meals he'd shared at Donna's table. They might not have been beef steaks, but they were just as tasty in their own way.

"The painting of the teepees intrigues me. The detail is fantastic."

Jim described the artist, and told how he'd bartered the paintings. "His family still maintains his wild horse herd. If you're in the market for a horse, they are the people you need to see."

Jeff was disappointed to learn the artist was dead. He was one person he would have wanted his classes to meet and get to know.

Chapter Thirteen

Thursday morning, while Jenny and Karl got ready to leave for Thanksgiving dinner with Karl's parents, Jeff placed a call to Illinois.

"I'm sorry I didn't give you my condolences yesterday when we talked on the phone," he said once he finished the pleasantries with his aunt. "I was so shocked, I forgot my manners."

"I understand completely. I'm just glad you returned my call this morning."

"I've been giving this a lot of thought and you must realize, I'm not coming to Illinois because of your father. I'm coming because of you and Uncle Paul. I've found a flight for tomorrow morning that should put me into Chicago at about one thirty. If you could get me a bus schedule, hopefully I'll be in Rockford in time for the visitation."

"You haven't booked the flight yet have you?" Kelly asked.

He could hear the tears in her voice. Had she changed her mind about him coming? "Not yet. I was planning to book it when I got off the phone from talking to you."

"Good. Your Uncle Paul has some frequent flyer miles on United he wants to use for you."

"That's not necessary. I can afford to buy my own ticket."

"Please don't, we want to do this for you. The tickets will be waiting for you at the airport in the morning. As for the bus schedule, that won't be necessary either. We're not having a visitation, so Paul and I will come down and pick you up. There's no use in arguing with me, because this is what we want to do for you. I realize this is your vacation and you'd planned to spend it with Karl and Jenny, but..."

"There's no need to explain. Besides my Uncle David and his

family, yours is the only family I have left. I've prayed about this and realized coming to Illinois is only proper. I'm not coming for the dead, but for the living. As for meeting me at the airport, I would certainly appreciate it, but I could also take the bus. Since I have to change planes in Denver it will be a long day."

"Good. Then we'll meet you in the baggage claim area for United just after one thirty. For such a short visit you won't have much more than a carry on, will you?"

Jeff wondered how he would get his suit in a carry on and still look presentable, but his aunt was right, he wouldn't need much for a two-day trip. "I have a bag I can use, but I'll need an iron once I get there, otherwise my suit will look like I slept in it."

With the phone call completed, Jeff took a moment to consider his decision. Last night he was prepared to say he wasn't going to Illinois. It wasn't until his Spirit Guide came to him in a dream telling him it was his duty to honor the past and his ancestors. Like it or not, his father's father was his ancestor, and to ignore the remainder of the family would be a dishonor to the man who had given him life.

"So, are you going?" Karl asked when Jeff came into the living room of the apartment.

Jeff nodded. "I was all set to say to hell with all of them, but then I realized I would be dishonoring my father. As much as I want to spend the weekend with you and Jenny, I know this is something I have to do."

"Good for you, buddy. While you were on the phone, I was doing some digging and I found this garment bag. It folds up so your clothes won't get wrinkled and will fit under the seat ahead of you. The rest of your stuff can stay here, and Jen and I will be happy to take you to the airport and pick you up on Sunday afternoon."

"Are you two ready to go?" Jenny asked as she joined them in the living room. "I promised Karl's mom I'd come out early and help her with the final touches for dinner."

Karl immediately got to his feet and Jeff went into the guest bedroom to retrieve his coat. If he knew the way out to Karl's parents' place, he would have opted to stay here and come out later. He wished he had some time alone to contemplate everything he'd experienced in the past two days. Maybe he would get the alone time he desired on the flight to Chicago tomorrow.

* * * *

The men of the Rivers family were enjoying the Thanksgiving Day football game while the women worked in the kitchen.

"So how is it going up at the reservation, Jeff?" Karl's dad asked.

"I'm enjoying it. The kids are great. I'm rooming with the shaman, so it feels like home when I lived with my grandfather."

"Well, you don't look like you're starving to death. My wife has been worried sick about what you've been eating."

Jeff again thought about the meals he'd eaten at Donna's table. "I have quite a great living arrangement. Alan, he's the shaman, takes his evening meals with his daughter-in-law, Donna, and her family. Since I'm rooming with him, I get my meals there as well. For breakfast and lunch, Alan and I share the cooking responsibilities. I'm far from starving."

"I haven't gotten him to tell me much about the people there," Karl added. "I'm more interested in his love life than his eating habits. Is there someone special?"

Marie's face flashed in his mind's eye. "I haven't had much time for romance," Jeff confessed. "Alan's granddaughter, Marie, teaches science at the same high school where I teach history. We haven't explored anything other than the things we have in common. I do know she doesn't have a special guy in her life."

Karl's mother called for everyone to come to dinner changing the conversation from Jeff's love life to the reasons everyone was thankful. While Karl's family was thankful for everything from food to family, Jeff mentioned his job rather than the Spirit Guide who'd become his constant companion in the past few months.

Even though the men were missing their football game, no one complained as the quality of the food drove even football from their minds. If Jeff thought he'd overeaten the night before, today he stuffed even more food into his ever expanding belly.

* * * *

Even though Jeff thought he was going to get solitude on the plane, he was sadly mistaken. It was just his luck that his seatmate from Helena to Denver was also traveling on to Chicago. She was an older woman who talked nonstop about her children and grandchildren. At least he didn't have to keep up his end of the conversation other than having to say yes or no in the right places now and then. She made it a point to sit next to him in the Denver airport and again, once they boarded the next flight.

When they finally arrived in Chicago, Jeff outdistanced the older woman and followed the other passengers heading toward the baggage claim area. If he was taking the bus to Rockford, he would have been able to make his way to the terminal from there.

While the other passengers waited for their luggage to come around on the conveyer belt, he left the crowd behind, easily recognizing his aunt and uncle standing near the stairs as well as the escalators leading to the main floor of the terminal. Even from this distance, he could see the strain of the past few days in his aunt's eyes. He didn't have to be a genius to realize Kelly and her father were very close. Why else would she have pressed so hard for Jeff to meet his grandfather last spring?

"Jeff, over here," Kelly called as she motioned for him to join them.

Kelly pulled him into a loving embrace, and he could feel her tears against his cheek. He knew they were a genuine outpouring of grief. He'd been too young to remember his grief at the loss of his parents, but the loss of his beloved grandfather was still an open wound in his mind.

"I know how you feel. At least I think I do. I felt the same way when I lost my grandfather last summer."

Jeff felt a man's hand on his shoulder and turned to come face to face with Paul Cooper. "I'm glad you were able to make it back here for the funeral," Paul said as he shook Jeff's hand.

"I'm in your debt for the ticket. I would have come even if you hadn't paid my way. Hopefully I can find a way to repay you."

"It's not necessary. I know what the starting pay for a teacher is. I've served on the school board long enough to be privy to that information. I realize our father did you, as well as your father, wrong. I loved my brother and we stayed in contact until the time of his death. After that, we lost all contact with you. I understand you know all of this, but I felt it was necessary for Wayne to be represented at the funeral tomorrow. We've been talking to several members of our family and

107

they're all anxious to meet you. I know how my father's will reads, I should I'm the executor of it. No matter what it says, I want you to have the portion of the inheritance that would have gone to your father."

Jeff swallowed hard. Before last summer, would he have been receptive to his uncle's offer? He doubted it. Even now, he wanted nothing from his grandfather, but doubted declining what Uncle Paul thought was his, wouldn't be easy.

"Let's get out of here. We've got a long drive to Rockford and if we hurry we can beat the rush hour traffic."

"Oh, Paul, get real," Kelly teased. "This is the Friday after Thanksgiving. The only traffic you will be encountering today will be the shoppers rushing home with their Black Friday treasures. Most people aren't even working."

The three of them shared a laugh before heading toward the tunnel leading to the parking structure. Within less than an hour, they were heading north along I90, and signs giving the mileage to Rockford were starting to be displayed on the overheads along the highway.

Kelly suggested he ride in the front seat with Paul, but Jeff opted for the solitude of the back seat of the SUV. In what seemed like the blink of an eye, he'd left behind the life he was accustomed to and entered the world of Kelly Grant and Paul Cooper.

Allow your white family to embrace you, Blue Eagle Feather, the voice of his Spirit Guide invaded his private thoughts. *Take what they have to give, and allow them to share your life. They are an important part of the future that is being woven for you.*

The realization of what his Spirit Guide was saying came as a shock. How could his white family be a part of the destiny his Spirit Guide predicted?

By the time Jeff regained his perception of the present, and what was going on around him, Paul pulled into the driveway of a well-kept older home in an established neighborhood. As Jeff looked at his surroundings, he realized there were several cars parked on either side of the street surrounding the residence.

"It looks like everyone is here," Paul announced. "The family is excited to meet you."

Jeff cringed at his uncle's pronouncement. He was here for his aunt and uncle. Meeting the rest of their family wasn't his top priority. Maybe in the future, but not after a long day of traveling.

Before Jeff could retrieve his carry on from the back of the vehicle, Paul had it in hand, and was heading for the front door of the house. For the first time, Jeff realized a light snow had begun to fall.

The snow is a sign. Its whiteness shows the past being covered, and the future is yet to be written upon the face of the earth. This new chapter is yours to write. Do so with care, and great things will be revealed.

"Jeff, are you all right?" Kelly asked, putting her hand lightly on his.

"Oh, yes, of course I am. I was just trying to put everything in perspective. From the amount of cars parked out front, I can only assume you have a large family waiting for me inside."

Kelly smiled. "We have three living aunts and four living uncles. They never agreed with the way our father treated your family, but they could do nothing about it. They're anxious to meet you. Along with them are my kids as well as Paul's family."

Jeff nodded. Around him, the snow was beginning to stick to the grass even though the sidewalks and streets were still warm enough to melt it as soon as it fell. His Spirit Guide was right, this was a new chapter in his life, and like the chapter he was building in Montana, it was his to write.

When Jeff entered the house, he felt the emotional embrace of the people waiting to meet him. These were people who had been important to his father when he was growing up, as well as when he married someone his parents didn't approve of.

Many of the older women cried when he was introduced to them. "You look so much like your father, the woman he now knew as Aunt Norma said. "His mother was my sister, and I cried the day she told me they'd decided to disown him because of the woman he'd married. I don't know how many times I begged her to give me an address so I could keep in touch, but she said this was their decision, and I should keep out of it. What I really think is it was your grandfather's decision, and she didn't want to go against her husband."

Jeff swallowed hard. From his one meeting with the man who'd given life to his father, he'd realized whatever the man said was law, and no one dared to question him.

After he was formally introduced to his aunts and uncles, Jeff gravitated to the young people in the room. They were his cousins, some of them his age, and others the age of his students in Montana. He could relate to them much better than he could the older generation.

His cousins were the exact opposite of him. Their blond hair and blue eyes stood in direct contrast to his darker features. Although his hair wasn't as black as his grandparents had been, it was a very dark brown that matched his eyes. Even his darker skin made him stand out from the others.

The older cousins were polite enough not to ask too many probing questions. Unlike them, the teenagers and those who were younger, had many questions about the life he'd lived and was still living on the reservations. They were surprised to hear they had not only television and cell phones, but also internet access.

"I thought you'd be like the Indians I see on TV and in the movies," fourteen year old Rosalyn commented.

"Oh, Roz, you're such a twit," her brother Brad said, punching her lightly in the arm. "Even I know that's not the way things are anymore."

"Your sister makes a valid point," Jeff agreed. "Unfortunately, the picture everyone has about Native Americans is the one portrayed by Hollywood, be it in movies or on television. I live with one of the elders in a beautiful home where he raised his family with his wife. I don't live in a teepee, although when I was in South Dakota, I stayed in one during the pow-wow I attended. The school I teach at is quite modern, and the kids I teach are no different from you. On the first day I had to tell them to leave their IPods, tablets and cell phones in their lockers when they came to my class."

"And they did it?" Brad asked. "At my school everyone takes all those things to class."

"You wouldn't if you were in my class."

"So what is it you teach?" Roz questioned.

Jeff smiled at her question. "History, US history to be exact."

"How boring. My older sister told me she hated that class. There were just too many dates to remember. Do you make your students memorize all those dates and stupid wars?"

"We learn about the wars, but we also learn about what was going on with the tribes at the same time. The kids seem to enjoy the classes and so do I."

Before he could be bombarded with any more questions, Kelly came to get him for supper. The food was laid out on the counter in the kitchen buffet style, and by the amount of food, he was certain everyone had brought their specialty.

"I hope the kids didn't bug you too much. I know there are times when Roz can be a real nosey rosy."

"It wasn't a problem at all. I'm always glad to talk to kids. If I wasn't, I wouldn't make a good teacher. Besides it was a good chance for me to change some of her preconceived ideas about what life on the reservation is like."

His comments brought knowing smiles from the adults around him as if he'd given them the answers they wanted to hear.

Chapter Fourteen

The solitude Jeff craved on his trip to Chicago now overwhelmed him. Although the flights back to Helena were filled to capacity, his seatmate had no desire for conversation. Instead, as soon as they were settled into their seats for takeoff, the woman opened her book making it perfectly clear she wanted no interaction with those seated around her. Across the aisle, the man looked like a businessman, and as soon as the announcement was made people could turn on their electronic devices, he opened his computer and began working on something.

At first, Jeff embraced his private moments, but soon he realized he wanted to talk to someone about what he'd experienced in Illinois. The grandfather, who wanted nothing to do with him, rested quietly in the casket with a serene expression on his face. It didn't take much for Jeff to see the father he knew only from the pictures his grandmother preserved in the family album. He'd seen the same resemblance in both his Aunt Kelly and Uncle Paul. It amazed him to realize he hadn't noticed it back in May when he'd first met the family he'd had no contact with for his entire life.

The resemblance was only the first of the things that bothered him. The fact his Spirit Guide told him of his need to be with these people at this time, gave credence to both sides of his heritage. Why would his Spirit Guide be so adamant about this meeting?

Even though Karl and Jenny were meeting his plane in Helena, he knew he couldn't talk to them about the happenings of the weekend. His questions would have to wait until he was back on the reservation and able to talk to Alan privately.

With his flight so early in the morning, he'd insisted it wasn't necessary to take him to the airport as he could take an early bus to Chicago, and not cause anyone to take him there. Both Kelly and Paul protested, but he'd stood firm in his determination to take the bus back to the airport. He decided he needed the alone time the bus ride would give him. Now he wished he'd asked them go take him all the way to the boarding area.

"We will be landing in Denver in fifteen minutes," the voice of the pilot announced over the loud speaker. "We're experiencing turbulence, so we ask that you turn off your electronic devices, stow your tray tables and fasten your seat belts."

The announcement had no impact on Jeff's seatmate, but the man across the aisle reluctantly turned off his laptop and put up his tray table. Since Jeff hadn't unbuckled his seat belt during the entire flight, all he had to do was put up his tray table.

"Is Denver your destination?" the man across from him asked.

"No, I'm going on to Helena. How about you?"

"I've got a business meeting first thing in the morning. I wasn't happy about leaving on Sunday, but there was no other way I could get here in time."

Jeff nodded. "What kind of business are you in?"

The man went on to explain about the company he worked for, as well as the presentation he would be making. Jeff welcomed the diversion, especially since the man didn't ask him anything about his reason for going onto Helena.

After about an hour layover in Denver, Jeff boarded a much smaller plane heading to Montana. This flight was far from crowded, and Jeff had an entire row all to himself. Here he didn't think about his Spirit Guide. His thoughts were on Roz and her brother and the questions they had posed. He'd exchanged e-mail addresses with them, and promised to add them to his friends list on Facebook. Their questions reminded him of the ones he'd been asked by the members of his class, and wondered if he could set up a Skype chat between the two groups of young people. It was definitely something he wanted to share with his class, and get their input on such a venture.

His flight landed before he came to any concrete decision about his idea. It didn't take him long to deplane and head for the baggage claim area to meet Karl and Jenny.

"How was the family?" Jenny asked.

He knew she'd be anxious for news from home. Even though he was comfortable in his new surroundings, Karl told him several times of how Jenny was feeling homesick for the Midwest. After telling her about her cousins and others in her family, he turned the conversation to the amount of snow that had fallen since his departure two days earlier.

"We had one hell of a storm on Saturday. We got a good ten inches, but the streets were cleared this morning. I do worry about you heading toward the reservation today. I'm not sure how well they keep those back roads plowed."

Jeff contemplated Karl's comment. Once they were back at the apartment, Jenny served them a lunch of chili and ham sandwiches. While she was busy putting the final touches on lunch, he pulled out his phone and called Marie.

"Hi Jeff," she greeted him. "Are you back from Chicago yet?"

"I just arrived. My friends thought I should check on the condition of the roads out there. They're good here in town, but what about the back roads?"

"They're iffy. We weren't even considering trying to get out to the diner this morning. Thank goodness we aren't open on Sunday mornings during the winter. I'll talk to Grandfather and get back to you, but maybe it's best if you stay on in Helena overnight. That will give the snow time to either be cleared or melt. We're looking for the temperature to get up above freezing today."

"Thanks Marie. I'll give Alan a call as well. If I'm going to stay here overnight, he's going to have to arrange for someone else to take over my class tomorrow."

Alan said the same thing as Marie, but then added, "There is something weighing heavily on your mind, Blue Eagle Feather. Have you had further contact with your Spirit Guide?"

"I have, but it's nothing I can go into at this time. With winter coming, I'm sure we will have plenty of time to talk about this in the next few months."

After hanging up the phone, he turned to see Karl standing behind him. "Anything you want to talk about, Buddy?" Karl asked.

Jeff panicked. He'd said very little to his friends about the visions he'd been having. How could he open up to them at this late date? In no way could he expect them to understand all the things he'd been going through since leaving Wisconsin last summer.

"We roomed together for four years, Jeff. I know your moods all too well. Something is bothering you. I'm all ears. You listened to enough of my problems over the years. Maybe it's time to turn the tables."

"Maybe it is," Jeff agreed. "If I can't trust you and Jenny, I can't trust anyone."

For the next hour, his friends listened as Jeff told them about the visions he'd been having and the *man* name he'd received from his Spirit Guide.

"Blue Eagle Feather, I like that." Jenny seemed to look at him with new eyes. "It suits you. Have you discovered what it means?"

"Not yet, but Alan has promised to enlighten me sometime in the future. The fact I heard the voice of my Spirit Guide while I was in Illinois tells me I have something to do in my life, but I don't know what it is."

"Were you having a vision while we were out to eat the other night?" Karl asked.

Karl's question shocked Jeff. He was certain no one noticed the time he'd been lost in the vision at the restaurant. "I was. I saw the painting with the two teepees, and I was immediately inside of the one closest to us. I could see all the belongings of the people who called it home. It was as though I'd been in that teepee, perhaps even lived in it in another life."

Karl shook his head. "That is so deep. How in the hell do you live with it? I don't know if I'd still be sane if I started having visions and had no idea what they meant."

"I'm coping. In time I'm sure Alan will be able to explain it to me, but for now I'm dealing with it the best I can."

"Well, you're a better man than me. I'm afraid if I started having visions, I'd run off to the nearest nut house and check myself in."

Jeff laughed at his friend's comment. "I never considered doing anything like that. To be truthful, the visions intrigue me. I know they're a part of me, I just don't know what part they are going to play in my life."

"Do you think you're glimpsing your past lives, Jeff?" Jenny asked.

Jeff nodded. "I do. I've lived in this area in the past, and I'm sure I've been part of the native community. I believe I fought at the Little Big Horn, and I've hunted buffalo in the ancient way, much like those of my people who came before me. I'm even coming to the conclusion this is not the first time the eagle has been my Spirit Guide. I know this all sounds like a lot of craziness to you, but I'm learning this is part of my make-up, and I have to accept it."

Jenny came to his side and gave him a sisterly hug. "I'm pleased you felt comfortable enough to share this with us. It will be interesting to see what you larn when Alan is finally able to tell you what these visions mean."

Chapter Fifteen

"Are you leaving this morning?" Jenny asked during breakfast.

"I'd planned on it. I should be back home by noon unless I run into some bad roads."

Karl put down his coffee cup. "Jen and I were talking about this last night after you went to bed. Since I don't have to be at the hospital until three this afternoon, what do you say we go car shopping?"

Jeff was taken aback by his friend's question. "What do you mean? My car has a lot of good life left in it."

"Sure it does, but I've lived out here all my life, and if I were in such a remote area as the reservation, I'd want a four-wheel drive vehicle. While you were gone, we took your car to the Jeep dealership to see what kind of a deal you can get."

At first Jeff was miffed to think his friends had gone behind his back, but the more he thought of it, he realized they were right. Even as old as Marie's truck was it had four-wheel drive. Considering the unpaved roads in the area, a new vehicle was definitely a good idea.

"I hope this dealership has a used car lot. I'm not prepared to pop for a new vehicle right now."

"I checked that out too. I think I found exactly what you need. It's a sweet little 2007 Jeep Wrangler with low mileage. Since your car is paid for, I doubt you'll have to pay much difference."

Jeff didn't argue too much. Karl's idea about getting a different vehicle made sense. He'd seen enough of the unpaved roads to realize a four-wheel drive vehicle would be more practical than the car he was driving now.

By noon, rather than pulling onto the reservation, Jeff was just pulling out of Helena in his new Jeep. The fact the vehicle only had one owner was definitely a plus, and the low mileage made it appealing.

As soon as he pulled onto the first unpaved road, the four-wheel drive became the most important feature of his purchase. Snow still covered the road in many areas, and where it didn't, the melting snow had created muddy ruts.

He found Alan at Donna's house preparing to sit down to supper. He smiled to see a place set at the table for him. "Guess I didn't get here any too soon."

"We've been watching for you all day." Donna finished putting supper on the table. As she did, he saw her glance out the window. "Oh my, did you get a new vehicle? I don't see your car out here."

It pleased Jeff to think Donna even had time to notice the now muddy Jeep Wrangler parked in front of her house. "My friend, Karl, talked me into it. He thought I should have something with four-wheel drive. I tended to agree with him. It's not new, but it had only one owner, and the guy took great care of it. Besides, it was something I could afford."

Alan chuckled. "You'd better be careful. Some of those young bucks in your class would give anything to get their hands on your new set of wheels. You'd better keep it in the garage at night."

Jeff thought of the parking spot in Alan's garage where he'd kept his car ever since he arrived to start the school year. "The good thing about the Jeep is that it won't take up as much room as my other car did. It's really a blast to drive, and I certainly appreciated the four-wheel drive when I got closer to home."

The smile spreading across Alan's lips said volumes. "I am pleased to hear you refer to this as home. Most of the teachers we get through the scholarship program can only talk about what they will be doing as soon as their five-year contract is up. You've only been here a few weeks, and I've yet to hear of your future plans."

"I'm afraid my future plans aren't in my hands. To be honest, I'd hope to talk to you about everything once we were alone." He glanced around the table. As he did, he hoped Alan understood he didn't want to discuss any of this with Donna, Marie, and the children around.

Marie reached over and touched Jeff's hand. "I know you're anxious to talk to Grandfather, but I'd like to have a ride in your new vehicle. If I'm lucky. You might even let me take the wheel."

The offer Marie made overrode Jeff's desire to talk to Alan. Before answering Marie, he glanced at the man he'd come to look at as a mentor. The slight nod of Alan's head gave him the permission he felt he needed to spend some alone time with Marie.

"Late night expeditions are for the young," Alan commented. "As for me, I've been fighting a cold all weekend. I think I'll go home and turn in early."

* * * *

With supper finished, Alan insisted on helping Donna with the dishes while Jeff and Marie went out to the Jeep to take it for a drive.

"These are great wheels. How did it handle in four-wheel drive?"

Jeff relaxed, and sang the praises of his new toy. Even though evening had fallen along with the temperatures, the night sky was clear of clouds, and the full moon illuminated the countryside, accompanied by a myriad of stars.

They talked while Marie drove them to an area of the reservation Jeff hadn't been to before. To his surprise, in the clearing were two teepees that mirrored the painting he'd seen at the restaurant before leaving for Illinois.

"What is this place?"

Marie turned to him and smiled. "This is Grandfather's and my special place. It's where we come to seek guidance from our Sprit Guides as well as The Great Spirit."

For a moment, Jeff was speechless. He'd accompanied Alan and Marie to church services every Sunday since his arrival, and what she was telling him went against everything he knew about them, and their religious practices.

"Are-are you a shaman?" In the moonlight, he could see Marie nod her head.

"I've been training with Grandfather for several years. I had my first vision while I was in college. I was so spooked by it, I immediately called him, and he told me he'd been aware of my calling ever since I was born but knew the time wasn't right for me to know the truth."

119

"Then you know..." he left the remainder of his thoughts unspoken. By the expression on Marie's face, he realized she was well aware of the visions he'd been experiencing ever since leaving the security of his home in Wisconsin for the unknown of Montana.

"Yes, Jeff, or should I call you Blue Eagle Feather? I've known of your visions ever since the day you stopped at the café. I could see you were confused by them and yet anxious for more information."

"I-I didn't know there were female shaman. I thought...well, I guess I thought wrong."

"A female shaman is rare, but we do exist. Most of the ones I've read about were in either South America or Asia, but I'm sure the female healers of the North American tribes were shaman, but the men didn't want to acknowledge them as such. Grandfather was grooming my father to follow in his footsteps, but he was diagnosed with stage four pancreatic cancer. I was about ten at the time, and within three months of his diagnosis, he was gone. Grandfather mourned his death, and prayed about who would take his place after he too walked with the ancestors. The Great Spirit answered his prayers by telling him when the time was right, my powers would be revealed. That said, I've been studying with Grandfather ever since."

When the time was right. The words resonated within Jeff's mind. It was hard to believe, but maybe the powers that be, deemed the time was right for him. Could it be possible he'd been chosen to follow the ways of his grandfather and uncle?

Before Jeff could question Marie further, she got out of the vehicle and walked toward the second of the two teepees. Without question, Jeff followed her. Once inside, she switched on a flashlight. To Jeff's surprise, he realized it almost mirrored the interior of the teepee in his vision. He'd been here before, mentally, if not physically.

It took Marie only a moment to find a lantern she'd apparently left there in the past. It gave off enough light to make them comfortable to sit against the backrests in the lodge to talk.

"This is a typical shaman's lodge. Grandfather helped me build it, and furnish it in the traditional way."

"I've been inside here before, only just in my visions. I was in a restaurant in Helena, and saw a picture that mirrored these lodges perfectly."

Marie nodded. "I know the artist well. Grandfather told me he came here often, usually to sell horses, but Grandfather did bring him here. The painting is of these very lodges. It's no wonder you were able to see the interior in your vision. I feel you have been in one of these lodges before, when you lived another life as a shaman of your people."

Jeff contemplated what Marie said. "I don't know if I'm as certain of the future as you are. I know my grandfather was a shaman, and so is my uncle. I just don't think my mixed blood qualifies me for such a distinction."

"That's where you're wrong, Blue Eagle Feather. If you were unworthy, your Spirit Guide wouldn't have seen fit to give you your *man* name. It wasn't until I accepted my future that I received my *adult* name."

"Is it proper for you to tell me what it is?"

"You probably couldn't pronounce it in our native tongue. Loosely translated, it means Eagle Woman. It's no coincidence we share the same Spirit Guide. You were meant to come here, just as we were meant to meet."

Even though her confession confused him, Jeff accepted it, and took her in his arms. He'd wanted to kiss her ever since their first meeting, and now it seemed like the most natural thing in the world.

Chapter Sixteen

By the time Jeff returned home, the house was dark. Although he wanted to talk to Alan, waking the older man was out of the question. The mantle clock struck twelve times telling Jeff it would be a relatively short night. With all the happenings of the long Thanksgiving weekend, what he needed most was several hours of uninterrupted sleep, but in the morning, he would need to be up early to prepare for his students.

Instead of the peaceful sleep Jeff craved, it was disrupted with dreams of his paternal grandfather chasing him from the grave, demanding he renounce the name of Cooper and take on his maternal grandfather's name of Red Fox. He woke to the sound of his alarm going off far too early for his liking.

He was surprised when Alan decided to sleep in, but didn't begrudge the older man the opportunity. After fixing himself a breakfast of toast and coffee, Jeff left for his first day back in the classroom since the Thanksgiving vacation.

His first class greeted him with words of sympathy for the loss of his grandfather and lots of questions about his new vehicle.

Rather than tell them the truth about his relationship with his grandfather on his white side, he thanked them for their kind words and successfully turned the conversation to his Jeep.

A knock at the door interrupted them before he could get to the lesson plan. When he went to answer the door, he was surprised to see Marie standing there with tears running down her cheeks.

Leaving his class unattended, he stepped out into the hall. "What's wrong?"

"It's Grandfather. Mom went over there this morning to do the cleaning, and found him still in bed. He was burning up with a fever so she called the neighbor to help her get him to the hospital. She wants us to come over there to be with her."

"What about our classes?"

"The principal cancelled our classes, and we're to send our kids to study hall. This is important to everyone on the reservation. Grandfather is their shaman, and is well respected."

Jeff took a minute to go back into the classroom and send his students to the study hall for the remainder of the period. Once he was alone in the room, he put on his coat and prepared to meet Marie in the hallway.

By the time he joined her, she'd become more composed, although she looked as though the tears would start at any minute. Instead of going immediately out to his Jeep, he took her in his arms, and allowed her to cry against his chest. He honestly wished he could cry along with her, but his pride kept him from acting on impulse.

So much had happened in the past six months. He'd been on an emotional roller coaster, and now it seemed as though he was at the top of the ride, and waiting for everything to drop out from beneath him. Alan was the key to his destiny, and he certainly didn't want anything bad to happen to the old man he held in high regard.

"You're in no condition to drive," he finally told Marie. "We'll take the Jeep."

She made no protest to his suggestion, and meekly followed him out to the parking lot. It only took a few minutes to drive across town to the hospital. While he parked the Jeep, Marie went in to join her mother in the waiting room of the emergency area.

They were holding each other tightly when he found them. "Have you heard anything?"

Donna nodded. "He has pneumonia. They're taking him to a room. They told me they'd come and get me when he's settled."

He could tell by the look on her face, she didn't think the medical staff was telling her the entire truth. "Do you think the doctor would talk to me?"

Donna shrugged her shoulders. Even if she wasn't convinced about him being able to talk to the doctors, he went up to the desk anyway.

"Could I talk to Alan Turtle's doctor?" he asked the receptionist.

The woman looked up at him, and he could tell she was skeptical of his request. "Are you family?"

"No, I'm the new history teacher at the high school, and I'm living with Mr. Turtle."

"Oh, yes, I've heard about you. My brother is in your class. He calls you Blue Eagle Feather. I can't believe the change in him this year. He says it's all because of you. I'll see if Dr. Brenden is available to talk to you."

The thought that his notoriety gave him privilege bothered him, but at least he would be able to talk to the doctor in charge.

The receptionist took him into a private room, and told him to wait. It seemed like an eternity before the doctor finally came in to talk with him.

"So you're the infamous new teacher at the high school. Jackie, our receptionist has been singing your praises for months. I hear you're making a difference for your students. I'm Dr. Jake Brenden. Something tells me you're working here for the same reason as me."

"If you're talking about a scholarship, yes I am. I have a feeling the difference is that when the five years are up I'm considering staying." He knew his tone was close to being sarcastic, but he didn't care.

"That's where you're wrong Mr. Cooper. I've been here for eight years, and I'm not leaving any time soon. I just got married last year to a local girl, and I love what I do. Now, I'm told you're here concerning Mr. Turtle. Like I told his daughter-in-law, he has pneumonia. It's a mild case, but I'd like to keep him at the hospital for a couple of days for observation. It's a good thing she found him when she did. As soon as he's stable, you'll be able to go up to his room and see him."

Jeff thanked Dr. Brenden, and went back out to the waiting room to be with Marie and Donna. Marie was on her feet as soon as he came in the room. "Did you get to talk to him?"

Jeff smiled, hoping to put both women at ease. "I did. Dr. Brenden told me you're a heroine in this Donna. You found Alan before things got much worse. In reality he could probably go home, but they'd like to keep him for observation."

"When can we see him?"

"They'll let us know when we can go up to his room. For now, why don't we go down to the cafeteria, and I'll buy you both a cup of coffee?"

Being close to noon, the cafeteria bustled with the activity of the staff coming in for the first lunch shift. Along with the coffee, Jeff insisted they should all eat something in preparation for the long afternoon ahead of them. For himself, he chose a ham salad sandwich, and a cup of the potato soup. Each of the women picked up salads along with a cup of the soup.

"I'm worried," Donna declared when they were seated at a table in a secluded corner of the dining room. "In all the years I've been part of this family, I've never known Alan to be sick. What if…"

"Don't talk that way, Mom. Nothing can keep Grandpa down for long."

Jeff wondered if he was the one who should be bringing common sense into this situation. "Pneumonia can happen to anyone. As I recall, there was a girl I went to high school with who suffered with it ever winter. With all the modern medicine they have now, he should be better in no time." He was pleased what he said seemed to calm the women sitting with him at the table.

By the time they finished their lunch, Jeff was certain Alan would be settled in his room, and they would be able to see him. It was apparent both Donna and Marie were worried about what they would find when they got to the room where Alan was probably now resting, and getting the medication needed to fight the pneumonia.

As soon as Jeff entered the room, he felt his heart drop into his stomach. Alan lay in the sterile white room with a nose cannula supplying him with oxygen, while an IV pumped medication into his veins. Before he could even speak, he could hear Donna and Marie crying.

"I see no need for tears," Alan said, holding out his hand to his daughter-in-law and granddaughter. "It was a blessing you came to check on me this morning, Donna. I'm getting the care I need. Even though I am a shaman, this is something even my prayers could not heal. The doctors and nurses in this hospital are well trained, and will take good care of me."

"I was so worried, Grandfather." Marie took Alan's hand, and held it close to her heart.

"You have no need for worry. I am more concerned with the fact you and Jeff are neglecting your duties at the school to be here with me."

Jeff smiled to think even though his older friend was sick, he was thinking of their obligations at the school. "Our classes are getting in an extra study hall today. For many of them it will help them with their assignments when we're back at the helm tomorrow." He knew the words sounded hollow, but realized they were the ones that needed to be said to put everyone's mind at ease. In his heart, he needed to speak to the doctors before he would be comfortable with the situation at hand.

He stepped to the side, and allowed the two women to have their time with Alan. As he did, the room changed before his eyes. In the vision, he stood before the two teepees he'd visited with Marie the night before.

Your time has come, Blue Eagle Feather. The visions you have been having are only a prelude to the destiny you were sent here to find. Alan's time with the people is coming to an end. The future belongs to the young. For many years to come, you and Eagle Woman will lead these people into the future. It is no coincidence you share the eagle as your Spirit Guide. Eagle Woman has been destined to be in your life, and will help you bring forth your powers.

"Jeff? Are you all right?"

He blinked his eyes several time to refocus on the hospital room. Once he became more grounded, he found himself looking into Marie's concerned eyes. "I-I'm fine I think."

"Do we need to call the doctor?" Donna voiced her concerns.

From the bed, Jeff could hear Alan laughing. "You have lived around shaman for many years, Donna, and yet you do not recognize when someone is entranced in a vision. Even you, Marie, should have noticed Jeff was having a vision. Have you learned of your destiny, Blue Eagle Feather? When I have recovered from this set back, you and I will have some serious discussions about your future."

Jeff could only nod his head in agreement with what Alan said. If the vision he just experienced was right, his life was about to change drastically. With Alan's care entrusted to the hospital staff, being alone for a while was what he deemed necessary at this time.

"I think you need to rest more than you need to entertain company. I have something I should do. Do you think you can get a ride home with your mom, Marie?"

"I could, but do you need me to come with you?"

Jeff shook his head, and left the room. He needed some time alone to think. Last night he'd seen dry wood in one of the teepees, and knew it was ready to be piled in the fire pit to add warmth to the structure.

The drive to the secluded area he'd visited with Marie last night took almost forty-five minutes. Jeff smiled when the two teepees came into view.

"Am I ready for this?" he verbally implored his Spirit Guide. "In all my life I've never seen myself in the role of shaman. That is for men like my uncle and my grandfather. I am not worthy."

The silence surrounding him brought no answers. Rather than wait in the chill of the November day, Jeff entered the teepee, laid the dry wood in the fire pit and started a fire. It didn't take long for the wood to catch and take the chill off the interior of the structure.

Smoke trailed up through the smoke hole at the top of the teepee mesmerizing Jeff into a trancelike state. In the smoke, he saw the people of old who called this land home from the beginning of time. Bits and snatches of the visions he'd been experiencing for the past few months, assaulted his mind, and combined with other visions of the past.

You must learn from the past, Blue Eagle Feather. Once you know the history of your people, you will be better equipped to deal with the future of the people you have been sent to serve. You will become a shaman, a holy man, but not a healer. The days of the medicine man are over. The doctors of the whites bring much knowledge to the people. They will restore the health of the old man. It is like when your grandfather got sick. Native medicine could not have helped him, but the modern doctors prolonged his life until your education was complete.

Jeff felt tears rolling down his cheeks. They were the tears he'd been unable to shed at his grandfather's funeral. They were tears for the man who raised him, the parents who gave him birth, and the people who once lived on this land from the beginning of time, and now had lost that connection.

Tears are to cleanse your mind and soul. The days of old are gone. The future belongs to those who are your students. Give them the knowledge of the past, both of the people and of the whites. Then shape them into the leaders of tomorrow. You and Eagle Woman will join forces to teach these young men and women. The fate of the next generation is in your hands.

"Jeff, Jeff, are you in there?"

The sound of Marie's voice broke the connection with his Spirit Guide. "I'm here," he called getting to his feet. Before he could leave the warmth of the lodge, she entered to join him.

"I thought I'd find you here. Mom got worried when you didn't come home for supper, so I told her I'd come out here, and see if I could find you."

"How did you know I'd be here?"

"To begin with, you weren't at Grandfather's house. Besides, when I need to be alone, this is where I come. Have you gotten any answers?"

Jeff nodded. "There is a reason I came to this reservation at this time. The students are the future, and it will be up to you and me to put them on the right path. I still have much to learn, but with the help of you and your grandfather as well as our Spirit Guide, I'm sure the journey will be an interesting one."

In the light from the fire, Jeff could see Marie's smile coupled with her tears. It took only a moment for him to take her in his arms. Rather than the comfort he'd planned to give her, he realized how perfectly she fit in his embrace. It wouldn't do for him to move too quickly. That said he knew in time they would become a couple, and spend the remainder of their lives together.

Chapter Seventeen

Jeff spent the next couple of days in the classroom while at night he sat at the hospital with Alan. Often he sat in the side chair while Alan slept. He knew often Alan didn't know of his presence, but he still felt compelled to be there. This old man had come to represent the grandfather he'd spent so little time with while he was away at college.

Oh Grandfather, he silently implored, *I missed so much by going away to school.*

What you don't understand, Jeff, is that to fulfil your destiny, you needed the education only the university could give you. You now have the tools to face the future.

Jeff jumped at the sound of his grandfather's voice in the confines of his mind. He must have fallen asleep, and only dreamed the voice he so longed to hear again.

"You sit by my bedside again." Alan's voice came as a surprise.

"I thought you were sleeping."

"I have done a lot of sleeping, but I have always felt your presence at my bedside. Why do you stay with me when there is much you should be doing for your classes as well as your destiny?"

Alan's use of the word destiny mirrored what he'd heard his grandfather say only moments earlier.

"What should I be doing? What is my destiny?"

"Oh, Blue Eagle Feather, I think you know the answer to your question. In less than a month, there will be a conference of shaman here. I know I will be unable to take as active a part in it as I would have before becoming sick. My Spirit Guide has told me you have accepted the fact you were born to be a shaman. Do you think by sitting in my

129

hospital room the knowledge you need will come to you?"

The old man's words hit home. "I don't know what I expected, but I wasn't with my grandfather for the last four years of his life. I thought I would have more time with him, but…"

"You feel as though you let him down. Believe me when I say, no matter how much time you have with someone you love, it's never enough. I felt the same way when I lost my parents, my son, and my wife. It's always the same. You wish you had one more day, said one more thing, or weren't so busy with your life. It doesn't matter who you are mourning, it's always the same. Be it the Christian God or the Great Spirit, the number of days you have on this earth are determined at your birth. I know you loved your grandfather, but your presence would not have prolonged his life. Live for yourself. Whatever you have to say to your loved ones has been said many times before. One more time makes no difference."

Jeff nodded. He knew everything Alan said was true, but he still felt compelled to be at the old man's bedside whenever he could.

The announcement that visiting hours were over echoed through the rooms and hallways of the hospital. "I guess it's time to go. I'll see you tomorrow."

"I'd rather you take the time you would be here for mediation and study. There are many books in my library I think you will find of help in your quest for your destiny."

Leaving the hospital, Jeff was torn as to where he should go. He thought about going to the sacred teepees, but since the weather had turned bitterly cold, he opted to go to the warmth of Alan's home.

After checking the refrigerator, he realized they'd become so dependent on Donna for their evening meals, there was little real food in the house. After making himself a peanut butter sandwich, he went into the library.

The room was filled with floor to ceiling bookshelves, as well as a working fireplace. He sat the plate with the sandwich along with a glass of milk on the coffee table in front of the comfortable overstuffed chair, and started a fire. It didn't take long for the dry wood Alan kept in a basket beside the fireplace to catch and begin to burn.

Accompanied by the crackling of the fire, he perused the titles of the books. Among the hardcover and paperback books was a three ring binder that caught his attention. Pulling the binder from its resting place, he saw a beautifully illustrated cover, depicting a dream catcher in the foreground with the sacred teepees behind it.

Going back to his makeshift supper, he made himself comfortable in the chair, and opened the binder. In the neat handwriting he recognized as belonging to Alan, he began to read the old man's thoughts on his life as a shaman.

The first thing to catch his attention was the Blackfoot color wheel. With different colors depicting the four directions, the center color that of the Creator, was what drew Jeff in. The center color was blue. It qualified his name of Blue Eagle Feather as denoting his connection not only with the eagle as his Spirit Guide, but also the Creator.

Before he could read further, he became engulfed in a powerful vision. In it, his soul was waiting to be born. *Around the unborn soul were the powerful Spirit Guides of the people. The eagle, wolf, and owl all vied to be the Spirit Guide for his soul.*

"As his Guide," the owl stated, "he will carry the wisdom of the ages."

The wolf stepped forward. "With me as his Guide, he will have the courage to deal with everything the modern world will dish out to him."

Finally, the eagle had his say. "I am the most powerful of all the Spirit Guides. I have the courage of the wolf, the wisdom of the owl, and I can soar to heights never before reached. I will be the Guide for this soul. With me directing his life, he will change the future of the people, and lead them in not only a peaceful, but also a profitable future."

Around him, all the Spirit Guides voiced their agreement with what the eagle said. Proudly, the eagle flew over the soul as it began its journey toward life. As it did, the voice of the creator added credence to the choice of Spirit Guides for this child. "He is to be guided by the eagle, but he will also be my child to protect and love."

The vision faded only to be replaced with the sleep Jeff's body craved. Ever since Alan went into the hospital, his rest had been anything but refreshing.

* * * *

"Jeff, Jeff, are you all right?"

The sound of Marie's voice calling his name, jerked Jeff from his dreamless sleep. Beside him sat the untouched sandwich and milk. One sniff told him the milk was now sour, and the bread of the sandwich stale.

"I'm in here," he called, getting to his feet.

"My god, Jeff, you look like you slept in your clothes."

Jeff looked down at the rumpled shirt and jeans he'd worn since yesterday morning when he dressed for his Friday classes. "Guess I did. I went into the library to look at your grandfather's books and...and I had a vision. After that I must have fallen asleep."

"What time did you get home from the hospital last night?"

"Around nine, why?"

"Because it's one in the afternoon. If you got here by nine, you were probably asleep by ten at the latest. That means you've slept the clock around, and then some. Mom's worried about you not eating. She sent me over to make sure you hadn't starved to death, and to bring you back to the house for a good meal. That said, what are you eating?"

Jeff thought for a moment before answering. Since Alan went into the hospital, he hadn't had much of an appetite. "I usually have coffee and toast for breakfast and grab something at the school cafeteria for lunch."

Marie laughed at the description of his usual menu choices. "I've seen you in the cafeteria and I don't call a small salad and cup of coffee enough to run on. Grandfather told us you've been spending your evenings at the hospital, therefore, you haven't been coming over for supper I agree with Mom you need a decent meal."

Jeff agreed with everything Marie said, but eating was the last thing on his mind lately.

"Why don't you go and get cleaned up, and I'll pick up the remnants of last night's supper and then we'll go over to Mom's so you can get something decent to eat."

Jeff ran his hand over the stubble on his chin. The last thing he wanted was for Marie to go into the library, and find the spoiled milk and stale sandwich, but he also knew he needed to not only shower and shave but also brush his teeth. He was certain his morning mouth must have been enough to knock over a buffalo, to say nothing about offending Marie.

* * * *

After getting cleaned up, Jeff donned a pair of worn jeans, and a warm sweater before joining Marie in the kitchen.

"How many peanut butter sandwiches have you eaten in the past week?" she greeted him.

"Enough. We don't keep much of anything for proper meals in the cupboard. Your mother has us spoiled."

"I'll say. If this sandwich is any indication of the kind of meals you're fixing for yourself after you come home from the hospital, I agree with Mom. You didn't even touch the sandwich or the milk for that matter. I did see what you were reading. It seems you picked the perfect book to start with. Do you think it had anything to do with your vision?"

Jeff reviewed the vision and nodded his head. "In it I saw my soul before it joined with my body. Around it were three Spirit Guides; an owl, a wolf and an eagle. They were all presenting a case as to which one should be my Spirit Guide. It was the eagle who won out, and when he did, I heard the voice of the Creator."

The expression on Marie's face said volumes. "Wow, that's some vision. I don't know anyone who has ever heard the voice of the Creator. I think Grandfather is right, you are the chosen one to fulfill the prophesy of so long ago."

"I rather doubt that. I'm half-white. Somehow, I don't think I'm the one to play out the creator's plan. Let's change the subject. I'm suddenly so hungry I could eat your mother out of house and home."

Marie shook her head. "No matter how much you eat, you can't run away from your destiny. Sooner or later, you'll have to face up to it. Hopefully, Grandfather will be out of the hospital by then, and will help you through it."

Chapter Eighteen

A week after going into the hospital, Alan was released. Donna insisted on him staying with her until he regained his strength, leaving Jeff alone in the house. It gave him time to read more of the books in the library while planning the conference to be held between Christmas and New Years.

With permission from the school district, he was able to use the gymnasium for the conference and set up housing for the guests in the classrooms that would be outfitted with beds to be used in lieu of hotel rooms, which were practically nonexistent.

The excitement of Christmas was only a prelude to the conference. Although it was Alan's idea, he was far too weak to do any of the planning, leaving it to Marie and Jeff.

When he explained the conference to his classes, the boys as well as the girls volunteered to help in any way they could. While the girls offered to help with cooking of the meals in the kitchen of the school cafeteria, the boys helped turn their classrooms into dorm rooms for the visiting shaman.

On the day before the beginning of the conference, several vehicles caravanned from the reservation to Helena to meet the planes of the visiting delegates. For each shaman, a student was assigned as an angel to take care of all their needs while visiting the conference.

He was thankful the weather was cooperating, and since the storm in November, the temperatures had risen to near freezing without any snow or rain. It made it easier for the shaman to get to the conference.

Donna allowed Jeff to take her van to the airport so he could pick up not only his Uncle David and Aunt Betty, but also Ken and Chuck

Hawk. With him were Marie, Jason Wild Horse and Philip Wolf, the two boys who would be the angels for Hawk brothers.

"I hope we can pull this off," Marie commented as they pulled into the parking area for the airport.

"Everything should go off without a hitch. I think we've accounted for everything that could go wrong."

After parking the van, they waited for the other members of their party before going into the terminal to meet the flights coming from various parts of the country.

One by one, the flights came in, and the visiting shaman left with the young men who were assigned as their chaperones for the weekend. The last flights to come in were from Wisconsin and South Dakota.

Jeff was relieved to see both flights were on the same airline, making picking up passengers at the same baggage claim area easier. Ken and Charlie Hawk were the first to arrive. It surprised Jeff to realize he considered these men he'd met less than six months earlier almost like family.

"It's good to see you again, Blue Eagle Feather," Ken greeted him as soon as he entered the area.

"I've been looking forward to seeing you as well. Uncle David's plane should be arriving in about ten minutes, so once we get everyone's baggage we can head for the reservation. Ken and Chuck Hawk, this is Jason Wild Horse and Philip Wolf. They are two of my students, and will be your angels for the duration of the conference. If there is anything you need, just call on them and they'll get it for you."

"I'm concerned about Alan," Ken commented. "This conference was his idea. It's a shame he's not here to meet us."

"We thought the trip would be too much for him," Marie explained. "Since I've worked closely with both Grandfather and Jeff, I've come in his place."

Chuck nodded sagely. "Alan has told us of your abilities, and how he has trained you to be one of a very few women shaman in the country. He is so proud of you. We're honored to have you come to the airport to meet us. The last time I talked to Alan, he told me he was feeling much better, but I could tell he was not as strong as he was telling me."

Hearing his friends talking to Marie tore at Jeff's heart. In the few months he'd been at the reservation, he'd come to consider Alan in the same light as his own grandfather. He was so lost in his thoughts he didn't see his aunt and uncle until they stood in front of him.

"Something tells me your mind was a million miles away," Aunt Betty greeted him.

"I guess I was." He gave her a hug and then shook hands with Uncle David. "Living with Alan has reminded me of the years I lived with Grandfather, but didn't embrace all the things he had to teach me. I wish he could have lived to be with us at this conference. It would have meant so much to me to be able to tell him of everything that has happened over the past few months."

David smiled. "I'm sure he knows you have realized the extent of the powers you possess. I think this conference will be an eye opening experience for all of us."

Jeff was taken aback by his feelings for his aunt and uncle. David looked so much like Grandfather when he'd first taken Jeff in after the death of his parents. Memories flooded his mind as tears threatened to fall from his eyes. Until this moment, he hadn't felt the pangs of homesickness. He realized he'd been so caught up with his class, students and visions that came without warning, he'd given no thought to his Northern Wisconsin home.

"Are you okay, Jeff?" Betty asked her voice laced with concern.

All he could do was nod his head, for to speak the words aloud would bring on a flood of tears.

"We understand," David said consolingly. "I remember what it was like when I first realized my calling as a shaman."

"How—How did you know?"

David grinned, looking even more like Grandfather. "You must realize as a shaman, I know much of what goes on in the spiritual world. Your grandfather's spirit has been in contact with me. You have so much to learn. He has entrusted your training to those of us who are attending this conference. This weekend should be enlightening, not only to us but also to you and your students."

Jeff felt his body relax. "I wish Alan was well enough to be here. Thankfully, he'll be able to attend at least some of the workshops this weekend."

It took only a few minutes for the luggage from both flights to come around the carrousel. With each bag pulled from the conveyor belt, they were finally ready to leave for the drive back to the reservation.

Jeff was relieved when Marie insisted on driving back to the reservation, giving him a chance to relax and talk to David as well as Chuck and Ken.

* * * *

By the time they arrived at the reservation, the other cars from the caravan were parked at the school waiting for them to arrive so supper could be served. As they entered the cafeteria, the aroma of the venison the women were preparing made their mouths water.

The other attending shaman stood in groups getting acquainted. At the head table, Alan held court, greeting each of the participants as they came up to introduce themselves. David, along with Ken and Chuck made their way to the head table, leaving Jeff to hang back with the rest of the angels.

I don't belong with these men. They all know so much more than I do.

As soon as the thought popped into his head, he heard his grandfather giving credence to the calling Jeff received over the past several months. Rather than standing in the school cafeteria, he was in the sacred teepee surrounded by not only his grandfather, but also the great shaman of the past.

"Glean what you can from these men," a shaman from the past, wearing a headdress made from the head of a red fox said. His presence frightened Jeff. This man from the past was summing up the essence of this weekend.

"I am so proud of you, Blue Eagle Feather."

Jeff felt someone touch his shoulder, and turned to come face to face with his grandfather. The vision was not of the old man who breathed his last shortly after Jeff returned home. The man standing before him was the one who taught him to hunt, and told him of the Great Spirit and of God.

"Grandfather," Jeff managed to say before the teas of homesickness choked off any further words.

137

"I know your heart, my child. The name you've been given fits you well. You are the fulfillment of the long forgotten prophesy."

"What prophesy?" Jeff implored.

Before he could receive an answer, the men of the past disappeared from view, transporting him back to the cafeteria and the meeting he hoped would clarify the words of his vision.

Alan got to his feet and called for attention of the men and women gathered for the conference. "We have finally all arrived. This conference is something I have been wanting to put together for many years. Finally, the time is right. Before we begin, let us give thanks for God and the Great Spirit for bringing us together, and giving our women the food and the ability to prepare it for our substance."

With Alan's Native American table grace finished, people began to line up to fill their plates with the nourishing food on the buffet. It came as no surprise to see Donna fill a plate and take it to Alan. Even though he'd been home from the hospital for almost a month, the strength he once had, seemed to be non-existent.

Chapter Nineteen

The supper shared by the shaman the night before had been impressive, but it was nothing compared to the opening ceremony. Each shaman wore the regalia depicting his rank among those of his tribe. Jeff marveled at the beauty of each of the outfits, and realized his deerskin leggings and shirt paled in comparison.

David was the first to take the podium. "This weekend we are here to celebrate the legacy of being shaman. I come from a long line of shaman; my father, my grandfather, and each grandfather to come before us. I thought, perhaps, this line would be broken as neither my son nor daughter have shown any interest in what has been my life calling ever since I can remember. This past summer, my nephew, Jeff Cooper, began a journey I am sure he never expected to take. He has been receiving visions, and I have heard from many of you that you are also aware of what has been happening to him. The Great Spirit and his Spirit Guide have made themselves known to him, and given him the *man* name of Blue Eagle Feather. Although he has much to learn, I am proud to present Blue Eagle Feather to the assembly as the newest of our number."

Jeff was stunned by his uncle's introduction. He'd had no idea the men and women gathered for this conference were aware of the turmoil he'd been experiencing over the past five months. Before he could make his way to the podium, the room exploded in applause, not only from the attending shaman, but also from his students and the other members of the community who were in attendance.

"I don't know what to say," Jeff began once he stood next to his uncle.

"I know what you are thinking. You do not feel worthy of what is your destiny, but you are more than worthy. Ever since I was with you in South Dakota this summer, my wife and I have been working on a regalia that suits your new status. It is our privilege and honor to present it to you and know you will wear it proudly throughout this conference."

From the corner of his eye, Jeff saw his aunt come onto the stage. She carried the most beautifully tanned leather shirt and leggings decorated with blue beading along with a headpiece of equal beauty made up of not only the beading, but also the rare eagle feathers he knew had been artificially tinged in blue.

"I don't know what to say, other than thank you. I will wear this with pride, and hope to learn more about my calling this weekend. You are right in saying I do not feel worthy of this honor that has been bestowed on me. You are all my superiors as well as my teachers. I cherish the opportunity to learn, and grow from this experience."

In the back of the room, he saw his students beaming at him, as well as Marie with tears in her eyes. He could feel the pride radiating from her as well as his students.

With the opening ceremonies finished, David suggested they go to his classroom so he could change into his new regalia before the first workshop of the morning began.

Walking into the room where he taught history on a daily basis, he felt as though he'd entered a luxury hotel room. Since he'd been at the airport picking up his aunt and uncle as well as Ken and Chuck, he hadn't seen the transformation done by the members of the community. The work they'd done was impressive.

"Do you know whose room this is?" he asked.

David smiled knowingly. "It's the room Ken and Chuck are sharing. They knew we were doing to do this and insisted you change in here."

Jeff went behind the changing curtain, and took off the regalia he'd worn for the day, and put on the new garments he'd received from his uncle just moments earlier. As soon as he put on the new clothes, he felt his spirit change immediately. The vision of the shaman of the past repeated itself, telling him to listen intently to everything that was said and taught throughout this weekend.

With no mirror in the room, Jeff could only imagine how he would appear to the people gathered in the gymnasium. As soon as he stepped around the curtain, the look on his uncle's face said volumes.

"What a transformation," David gasped. "I see not only my father, but also my grandfather in you. I also see your father, the way he looked when he first came home with your mother, and told my father he wanted to marry her. It was hard for him to accept them as a couple, but in no way would he deny your mother that which was her heart's desire. To see you today, he would know he made the right decision."

Before going back to the gymnasium, Jeff stopped at the boy's bathroom to check out his appearance in the mirror. To his shock, he saw a powerful shaman in place of his usual reflection.

* * * *

When Jeff entered the gym, he saw a drum with the singers around it. The room resounded with the beat of the music, and the rhythmic singing of the men seated around it. People sat around the sacred circle watching the shaman who performed the purification ceremony. The scent of sage filled the air as tobacco was offered to the four directions as well as to the center of the sacred area depicting the earth.

An older shaman from Colorado, who Jeff knew as John White Horse, took center stage as the master of ceremonies. "This morning's session is a lesson from the past," he began. "In order to conquer the future, you must understand the past."

Using a cane, Alan joined John on the makeshift platform in the middle of the sacred circle. Jeff was relieved to see someone remembered to bring in comfortable chairs for the older men to use for the presentation.

"I am Alan Turtle, and for many years I have been the shaman of this reservation. When I was younger than most of the students at the high school, I went on my vision quest, and was given the name of Wise Turtle. The turtle has been my Spirit Guide. That is why it came as a surprise when my granddaughter Marie was given the name of Eagle Woman by her Spirit Guide, the Eagle. We were blessed when the Great Spirit sent Blue Eagle Feather into our midst, for these two, who are guided by the Eagle, represent the future of our people."

"I too am an elder from my people. My name is John White Horse, but from my vision quest, I learned my name is Grey Wolf. With that

141

name and persona I have led my people for many years. I have been told your assignment has been to make a plan for the future. I have read over your plans, and before we discuss them we will learn of the prophesy for the past that speaks openly to the future that lies before us."

One by one, other shaman joined Alan and John to tell the story they thought the people watching the ceremony should know.

"Long before the coming of the white men, there was a great shaman called Soars With Eagles. He received his name because of his ability to change his shape. In the times he was in contact with the Great Spirit as well as his Spirit Guide, he would become an eagle, and fly to the top of the mountains to commune with his Spirit Guide."

There was an audible gasp from young and old alike among the spectators. Jeff knew none of them would have expected to be hearing about the paranormal things they read about in books.

Once the murmurs quieted down, the next speaker began. "Soars With Eagles returned to his village from one such journey with a prediction of the future. He told the people he saw invaders coming to the land. These men and women would have skin of white as well as black, and many shades in between. The people scoffed at him, and said they'd heard of no such manner of men. It was then he left his people and journeyed to another village. He made his home with a different people who he prayed would believe the prophesies he made. So terrifying were his premonitions, he felt the need to warn all the people of the coming of these strangers. He foresaw them taking possession of the land that had been theirs since the beginning of time."

Another shaman picked up the narrative. "If the people in the next village questioned the first prophesy, they were wise enough not to vocalize their doubts. It wasn't until he predicted a great war with the invaders that the people lost confidence in him."

Again, the microphone was passed to the next man. "Soars With Eagles predictions were kept alive by the shaman to come after him. Throughout the years, each of these predictions came true. The last, and most important one was not fulfilled, and therefore all but forgotten. Soars With Eagles predicted, on his deathbed, that the day would come when the people no longer lived off the land. The people would become dependent on the whites, and would turn to the strong drink provided by their so called protectors, and would also become lazy."

Jeff noticed several people looking from one to another with knowing expressions on their faces. The poverty of the reservation combined with the problem of alcoholism that had taken so many lives gave credence to the prediction of the past.

"Soars With Eagles final prophesy was twofold The last part speaks of a great shaman who will be sent to the people. This shaman will have his feet in two worlds, that of the whites and that of the people."

The realization of the magnitude of the prophesy struck Jeff like a slap in the face. The sacred circle of shaman faded and was replaced by a vision of an eagle gliding toward him. Once the eagle was close to him it became one of the ancient shamans he'd seen previously.

I am Soars With Eagles. You have been carefully chosen, Blue Eagle Feather. You are He who I saw in my final vision. You have been sent here to shape the lives of the next generation. Use your gifts well, Blue Eagle Feather.

Unlike the other visions he'd encountered in the past, as it faded so did Jeff's conscious thought. His physical world went dark, but his spirit flew with that of Soars With Eagles. With the old man, he moved above the cold winter day, and the conference of shaman to the heights of the mountains.

This is your legacy, Blue Eagle Feather. This is the land of both the people and the whites. You must bring the two together, and insure the prosperity of the people who belong to both sides of your heritage.

* * * *

"Jeff, Jeff, can you hear me?" The voice along with someone tapping his cheek dissolved the vision, and brought him back to reality.

He allowed his mind to clear before opening his eyes. When he did, he not only saw Marie but also David and several of the other shaman kneeling at his side. In the background, he could hear sirens indicating the approaching of the paramedics.

"We were so worried," Marie said, tears running down her cheeks.

"It-it was a vision. A terrifying and exciting vision," he finally managed to say.

"Of all people, we do understand," David said. "We all agree you should allow the paramedics to check you over. From what you've told us, you've been experiencing many of these visions since you left Wisconsin. It's better to be safe, and check things out since this time you passed out and were unconscious for several minutes."

"I've been with you when you've had several of these visions. Never before have I seen you lose consciousness. Was that what you meant when you said this one was terrifying?" He could see the concern on Marie's face.

Jeff closed his eyes as he remembered the vision. "Soars With Eagles came to me and with his help my spirit became linked to his and I became an eagle. Together we flew to the top of the mountains, and spoke with our Spirit Guide. Even if I don't want to accept it, I'm the shaman mentioned in the ancient prophesy. It's no coincidence I've been sent to this reservation at this time. I'm here to guide the young men and women in my class down a different path in life than the one walked by their fathers and grandfathers."

He paused and took a deep breath. Before he could continue, two paramedics entered the gym. "Where is our patient?" Jeff heard one of them say.

As much as he wanted to protest, David led them to his side. "My nephew passed out. I'd appreciate it if you'd check him over."

"Can you tell me your name?" The first paramedic asked. He looked enough like Phil Wolf, it was evident the two were brothers.

Which name? Jeff wondered. "My given name is Jeff Cooper but my *man* name is Blue Eagle Feather."

The answer seemed to confuse the young man who worked at attaching the blood pressure cuff to Jeff's arm.

"I didn't think anyone took that man name stuff seriously anymore," the other paramedic said. Although the young man looked to be a member of this band of Blackfoot, he sounded very skeptical of Jeff's answer.

Jeff was about to protest when he was told to be quiet so they could get a proper blood pressure reading.

Although the young man taking the reading called him Mr. Cooper, Jeff seethed inwardly. In his mind, he'd stopped being Jeff Cooper. In the few moments of unconsciousness he'd become one with Blue Eagle

Feather. His past life no longer mattered. The future loomed large on the horizon, not the half-breed he'd been, but the shaman he'd become.

"All of your vitals are normal, but we'd like you to go to the hospital to be checked out further."

Jeff stared at the young man in disbelief. "There's nothing wrong with me. This is a conference of shaman. All that happened was I had a vision and lost consciousness."

David's face mirrored his disapproval of his nephew's reluctance to go to the hospital. At the same time, he nodded his agreement with Jeff's ability to speak for himself.

Reluctantly the paramedics left Jeff to get to his feet. The experience shook him to the core. After feeling his spirit fly with Soars With Eagles, the floor beneath his feel felt alien.

"Oh Jeff, we were so worried about you," Marie said as she came to his side. "I've watched you have visions before, but never anything like this."

He smiled at her concern. "I've never left my body before. Soars With Eagles came to me and helped me to allow my spirit to leave my body. I've never felt so free in my life." He could tell by the look on her face she was skeptical, but he knew what he'd experienced. In time, he would convince her, his vision and out of body experience, was as natural as breathing.

With the excitement over, the morning's ceremonies continued. Throughout the midday meal, each of the visiting shaman came to him with words of congratulations and encouragement.

"I've believed in Soars With Eagles' prophesies all my life," Chuck commented as he sat down next to Jeff. "To see the final one come to light before my very eyes is more than I've ever hoped for. I'm looking forward to this afternoon, and the presentations from your students."

After lunch, it was the students' turn to take over the microphones. Each group presented their ideas for the future. Not only the shaman but also the elders of the reservation listened with interest to the plans the young men and women proposed.

Jeff marveled at the creativity of the kids who sat in his class day after day. Thinking back to the beginning of the school year, he saw the growth of these kids from day one. No longer did they wear dreads and ratty clothes. Their long hair was now braided in the traditional way, and their clothes were ones any mother would be proud to send them out into the public with. Today, they were all dressed in native regalia.

It wasn't only their appearance that was exciting, but also their ideas for the future. There were some that were fanciful and farfetched, but for the most part, they were ones the elders could agree with and easily act upon.

"If these are the representation of the future," Ken began, "I think our people can look forward to a comeback in this great nation. At one time, this land belonged to us and us alone. With the coming of the white man, we realized we were outnumbered, and gave into the strong drink they brought with them. Not only were we defeated militarily, we were demoralized. Today, I've heard from the next generation about their hopes, and expectation for what is to come. I feel programs like this one should be instituted in the high schools on every reservation in the country. Many of you have had a chance to talk to your 'angels' since your arrival. I'm sure you have learned about the interesting history program, Blue Eagle Feather, has been teaching. Along with the history of the white man, he's also taught the history of our people. My 'angel' tells me he's looking forward to the session on WWII where they will learn of the 'Code Talkers' from the Navaho nation. Thank you, Blue Eagle Feather, for leading your students in a new direction, and giving us this opportunity to meet and learn from one another."

Those assembled in the gym broke into wild applause, leaving Jeff at a loss for words. Once he composed himself, he stepped up to the microphone. "On behalf of my students, I thank you all for your participation in this event. Without my students, this wouldn't have been possible. They, rather than myself, are the ones who deserve your applause. The idea may have been mine but they were behind me all the way in the planning of this. They were the ones who transformed their classrooms into hotel accommodations, planned the menus, supervised the cooking, volunteered to be angels, and last, but not least, put together their proposals for the future. When I came here, they had no future. They didn't think they could make a difference, but from what we have heard today, they've changed their minds. Many of them will go on to college to make the difference in their lives, but many will also be starting cottage industries working with the crafters who are already established."

Again, the applause was deafening. Jeff smiled to know it wasn't for him, but for his hard working students. At this moment, he couldn't have been more proud if these were his own biological children.

Chapter Twenty

Jeff awoke in the afterglow of the success of Saturday's conference. The day ended with an evening of drumming and dancing. Singers joined the drummers, and told the story as old as time itself in their song. Even without the traditional fire in the sacred circle, the music as well as the dancers were inspirational.

It took a moment to realize someone else was awake and up in the house. Pulling on his jeans, he walked barefoot and shirtless into the kitchen. He smiled to see his Aunt Betty standing at the stove preparing breakfast.

"I didn't expect to see you up and about," he greeted her.

"Have you forgotten the church service set for eleven this morning? Your uncle is in the shower, and I was just getting ready to come into your room to wake you up."

"Church?" Jeff questioned, trying to get his mind to focus on the present and return from the world of Soars With Eagles. "Oh yes, church. What time is it?"

"It's only nine, so you have plenty of time to get ready, and to eat breakfast. I realize it was a late night last night, but this will be not only our Sunday service but the end of the conference."

He nodded. "I'll get cleaned up and be down as soon as I can."

Once back at his room, he laid out the regalia he'd worn the day before, and prepared to go to the bathroom for a shower and to shave in preparation of the morning.

"You put on a good conference," David said when they met in the hallway. "You made me as well as your grandfather proud. To be honest, I've heard of Soars With Eagles' predictions for years, but never did I think my own nephew would be the one to bring them to life."

"I know what you mean. I still can't comprehend it all."

With tears in his eyes, David placed his hand on Jeff's shoulder and nodded solemnly.

* * * *

The church service was like the one Jeff experienced in South Dakota. What began as the traditional service soon became so much more. Photocopies of pages of hymns printed in several native languages as well as English were handed out. Rather than singing to either an organ or a piano, the music was provided by drums and flutes.

Each shaman sang the song in his native language, and then the congregation sang it again in the more familiar English. With David's urging, Jeff and Betty joined him in singing the words in Chippewa when their turn came. Although he rarely spoke in the language of his grandfather, Jeff found the words came more easily than he expected they would.

Around him, the people he now called friends mingled with students and shaman all intent on worshiping God each in their own way.

The service ended with prayers for safe travel for the shaman who would be returning to their homes as well as hope for guidance for the future. With the end of the service, men and women alike had tears in their eyes for all they'd experienced over the past two days.

"You must work hard to learn the language of the Blackfoot," Marie suggested, once they bid good-bye to all but Betty and David. "You have such a wonderful singing voice, it's a shame you do not lend it to the songs of my people."

"Do you have any suggestion as to who might be willing to be my tutor?"

David laughed at his question. "I think this young lady will be more than willing to tutor you in more things than language. I'm very impressed with your status as shaman, Marie. I've heard of women shaman, but never met one before. I doubt it's a coincidence both you and Jeff share the same Spirit Guide, and are in the same village. I have a feeling you will play a big part in the future Jeff will be shaping."

"I never thought about it that way, but perhaps you're right. Jeff and I have had a strong connection since the first time we met. The only future I could think of then was one I hoped to have with him as husband and wife. After this weekend, I know we are destined not only for that, but for much more."

Hearing Marie speak so frankly about her feelings for him took Jeff by surprise. He'd had the same feelings and intentions, but before now, he'd not voiced them aloud. Knowing he was not alone in his feelings brought thoughts of a bright future for the two of them.

* * * *

David and Betty stayed until New Year's Eve. Having his uncle with him, David asked more and more questions in the hope of getting the answers he desired. Alan and Marie insisted the four of them go up to the teepees while Betty spent the day with Donna.

"These are impressive," David commented. "Is it just me or do you feel the magic in this place?"

Jeff nodded. "I felt it when I first saw it depicted in the picture in the restaurant in Helena. I was immediately transported inside and saw all the trappings it contained. Imagine my surprise when Marie brought me here for the first time."

"Then you've had visions here?"

"I most certainly have."

"I suggested building a third teepee next summer," Alan interjected.

Alan's announcement of building another teepee brought forth a vision—one Jeff neither wanted nor accepted. In it, he saw Alan's death before the end of the coming year. With his passing, there would be no need for the third teepee. What once belonged to the old shaman would soon pass to him.

"No," his spirit screamed, but his Spirit Guide silenced his protests.

"Each life is allotted so many days. Those of Painted Turtle are coming to an end and you and Eagle Woman have been sent here to carry on his legacy."

"I am not ready for such a thing. I'm not worthy."

"Your worth has been tested. You will bring these youths into a time of prosperity. Follow your heart, and all will be as the Great Spirit has planned. The time for the fulfillment of Soars With Eagle's prophesy is at hand. Your destiny was cast on the day you were born."

150

The vision faded with none of the side effects he'd experienced at the conference only days earlier.

"Your vision was a powerful one," Alan commented once Jeff returned to the present. "It is one I have prayed the Great Spirit would send to you."

"H-how do you know what I saw?"

"I know because I saw it as well. I know the days of my life are numbered. I have known this since before you arrived and the Great Spirit and my Spirit Guide foretold not only your coming, but also your connection to Marie, and the end of my time here. I was promised a great shaman would come to take my place, and be the fulfillment of Soars With Eagles' prophesy. You and Marie will do great things for the people. Use your skills wisely."

Jeff tried to hold back his emotions but was unsuccessful. Facing the end of Alan's life brought back the loss of his grandfather six months earlier. He'd tried to be strong at the time, but in reality he'd been devastated. It had been in private that he'd shed the tears he felt were unmanly. Now they came without prompting.

"I wondered how long it would be before you were able to grieve for Father," David commented. "I was worried about you at the funeral and afterward. We all know death is a natural part of life, but for those of us left behind it is overwhelming. No matter when it happens or how it happens, remember those we lose have fulfilled the lifetime allotted to them at birth. Even though their physical bodies are no longer with us, their spirits linger forever."

Jeff nodded his head in understanding. He'd not only felt his grandfather's spirit around him, now through his visions, he'd been able to speak with the man who'd raised him with love and understanding. Even if his grandfather had known of Jeff's bright future, he'd never pushed him toward something he had no idea he wanted.

Chapter Twenty-One

Throughout the winter, when Jeff wasn't teaching, he played the role of student, learning everything he could from Alan. At the old man's insistence, Jeff took over the shaman's teepee, and spent many hours there in meditation and prayer.

During those time of solitude he often connected with Soars With Eagles, and found each time it was easier for him to leave his body behind and become an eagle. Although he didn't believe in shape shifters, his spirit seemed to have a mind of its own. In the moments and hours when he became an eagle, he spoke with many shaman from the past including his grandfather.

Why didn't you tell me of this Grandfather?

You were not ready. Had it not been for the visions granted you by the Great Spirit and your Spirit Guide, you would have been skeptical of the path your life would take. Among shaman, you are destined to be one of the greatest shaman ever to be. Your powers will rival even those of Soars With Eagles.

I fear I have not trained enough for this. Isn't it something I should have been doing all my life? I should have listened more to what you had to teach me. I missed so much by not learning from you.

Had I known your destiny while I walked the earth, I might have pressed harder, but it was not until my Spirit Guide and the Great Spirit joined, that I learned of the life you will be living. Painted Turtle is an excellent teacher. Even though his time here is limited, he will give you a good foundation. His granddaughter, Eagle Woman, also has been sent to help you along your way. Rest assured, you will soon far exceed the abilities of either one of them.

Jeff awoke with a start. With each communication with the great shaman of the past, he knew he would return to familiar surroundings completely and utterly exhausted. He was always glad his periods of unconsciousness never happened in the classroom. His students had been frightened enough by the one he'd suffered at the conference.

"I thought I'd find you here."

Jeff looked up to see Marie enter the sacred teepee. "Something tells me your mother has supper ready, and as usual I'm going to be late again."

Maria laughed. "Not this time, Big Boy. Mom sent me out here earlier than usual. Considering this is spring break, she knows where to find you. She said to tell you I came early so your supper wouldn't get cold this time."

"I'm becoming a creature of habit. What would you say if I asked you to break out of the routine and go to Helena with me this weekend?"

"Are you going to see Karl and Jenny?"

"We can but there's a shop I'd like to visit. I know this isn't the proper time or place, but my Spirit Guide and the Great Spirit both assured me you are an important part of my future. I'd like to make it official, and ask you to be my wife."

With a minimum of steps, Marie crossed the distance between them, and allowed him to take her in his arms. "I've know we were destined to be together ever since the first time we met. I'd be honored to be your wife as long as you don't insist on a long engagement. I want Grandfather at my wedding, and I fear his prediction of death will soon come true."

Jeff reluctantly agreed with Marie. As much as he wanted to deny the old man's prediction, his many spirit journeys confirmed everything Alan told him. Life was short and precious, and like many of the men who came before him he knew his days were few in numbers.

"It's settled then. Let's go to your mom's place and start making plans. This weekend we can get the rings, and ask Karl and Jenny to come here for the ceremony. I can't imagine getting married without my best friend at my side."

* * * *

As soon as they entered Donna's kitchen, Marie blurted out the news of their engagement.

"I told you, Donna," Alan said with a wise wink. "I knew these two were destined to be together before Jeff came here to teach. I saw it in a dream more than a year ago. I hope you two are planning to marry soon as I want to take my son's place and give Marie away at your wedding. I am pleased with the union that will soon take place."

"I promise we won't wait long, Grandfather. Jeff is taking me to Helena this weekend to talk to his friends, and for us to pick out our rings."

All through dinner, the talk was of weddings. Jeff allowed the women to make the plans while he contemplated what he wanted the special day to include. He knew Karl would be surprised by the Christian and Native American ceremony he now heard Marie and Donna discussing.

"What do you think of Memorial Day weekend for the wedding?"

Marie's question broke into his thoughts on the wedding. "Are you sure you can be ready so soon? That's less than two months from now."

"Never fear, for the kind of wedding my daughter wants, we could do it tomorrow. Of course I know there are people you want here, and travel plans take time to make."

Jeff appreciated Donna's encouraging words. He did have several people he wanted to ask to witness his wedding. He also wanted his Uncle David to perform the Native American part of the service. This was going to be the most special day in his life.

* * * *

On Friday morning, Jeff and Marie left for Helena. He was pleased that Karl and Jenny wanted them to stay at their apartment. He'd worried about the cost of two hotel rooms, but with Marie using their spare bedroom, and him bunking on the pullout couch, the weekend would be completely on the up and up. Neither one of them believed in sex before marriage.

"So, what brings the two of you to the big city?" Karl asked as soon as they arrived.

"It's the end of spring break, so we thought it was time to do something special. Marie and I are planning to do some shopping, and we have an important question to ask you."

Jenny's eyes widened as she took Marie's hand in hers. As though disappointed not to see a diamond ring on the third finger of her left hand, Jenny cast a questing glance in Jeff's direction.

"The ring is the reason we're in town. That and to ask Karl to be my best man. Do you think you can get off for Memorial Day weekend?"

"You old son of a gun, why wait so long to tell us?"

Jeff smiled at his friend's question. "It would have been a little hard to give you much more of a head's up since Marie just agreed to marry me on Tuesday night. If you can make it, I'll start calling the family."

Karl pulled Jeff into a bear hug. "For you I'd move Heaven and Earth. I'm sure I can get it off especially since I'm signed up to work Easter, the Fourth of July and Thanksgiving. To be truthful, Memorial Day was the one holiday I have off already. Just tell us when and where and I'll get a tux."

"Not so fast. Marie has her heart set on a Native American ceremony. We'll just have to get you some regalia and you'll be all set."

While the girls talked weddings, Karl and Jeff shared a beer. "So life on the reservation must suit you well. Are you still convinced your calling is to be a shaman?"

"As much as I've tried to deny it, I'm sure the die is cast. We've got all weekend to talk about this. What say Marie and I take you two out to dinner?"

Jeff knew his suggestion hit a positive note with the girls. In no time at all they were headed to The Old Miners Dining Club. Because of the beer Jeff enjoyed at the apartment, Marie insisted on driving. He had to admit it was fine with him since he hadn't had more than one beer since Karl's bachelor party. The last thing he wanted was to get a ticket for drunk driving when he was telling his students to abstain.

At the restaurant, Marie was as taken with the artwork as Jeff had been months earlier. The fact she'd known the artist who made the paintings, made it even more special for her.

After staring at the painting for several minutes, she turned away with tears glistening in her eyes. "I was just a little girl when that picture was painted. He came up to see my grandfather right after the second teepee was erected for my father. The next summer my father died, and this is the first time I've seen the finished product."

"Are you saying these teepees are on your land?" Jenny questioned.

"Yes. One belongs to my grandfather and soon will belong to Jeff, and the other is my place for meditation and prayer."

"What do you mean your grandfather's teepee will belong to Jeff?" Karl inquired.

Marie paused for a minute to compose her thoughts. "My grandfather's days in this life are numbered. Jeff has been chosen to take his place as shaman."

Jeff enjoyed the expression of surprise on his friends' faces. When he first came to Montana, he'd been confused about his calling, even tried to deny it. With the recent changes in his life, he knew he'd been chosen at birth, and nothing he could do would change what both the Great Spirit and his Spirit Guide were working to bring about in his life.

* * * *

Once they were back at the apartment, Jeff knew both Karl and Jenny would expect a full explanation of what was going on, not only in his life but also on the reservation. They spent the rest of the evening with Jeff making a confession he never thought he would make.

It was hard enough for him to understand the ramifications of the visions, and out of body experiences he'd been having ever since summer. Telling his friends, and eventually the white side of his family was something he found very difficult.

"I can't believe I know someone who is a shape shifter," Karl said. "I remember reading a book about shape shifters in high school. I thought it was all part of the author's warped imagination."

Marie laughed at Karl's comment. "When Jeff talks about being a shape shifter, he doesn't literally change shape in front of our eyes. He goes into a trance, and his spirit becomes one with his Spirit Guide. It is his spirit that changes, not his physical body. I've been with him when this transpires, and have come to understand more of his powers because of it. The first time it happened was during the conference of shaman we held on the reservation over the Christmas vacation. It was very frightening and someone even called the paramedics. Even the visiting shaman had never seen someone go into such a trance before. We have all had visions, but this was very much different because he lost consciousness."

"Do you have these visions too?" Jenny inquired.

Marie smiled. "I have visions, but I do not have the same powers as Jeff. I've never left my body nor have I shifted in the same way he does. What you have to understand is that Jeff is a very powerful shaman. He is just coming to grips with his powers as well as the realization he is the fulfillment of an ancient prophesy. My grandfather insists he was destined to come to our reservation even before he was born."

"Then why didn't you know?" Jenny asked.

"I grew up in a shaman's house, but Grandfather never pushed me toward my Native American heritage. He felt I should follow in the footsteps of my mother and father rather than those of Grandfather and Uncle David. I doubt he had any idea of the powers I would develop once I moved to Montana."

"The old man was a great shaman," Karl said once Jeff stopped to take a breath. "I should know, I remember spending spring break with you and I was in awe of him. How is it he didn't know?"

Jeff smiled as he contemplated Karl's question. "I think it's because my Spirit Guide didn't make himself known until I was on my way to Montana. He put great people in my path to counsel me about what was going on in my life. It wasn't until I heard the ancient prophesy that everything became clear to me. Uncle David was with me and he, too, was amazed by what happened."

They talked long into the night, and Jeff revealed more of the things he'd experienced in the last few months. Even though he'd lived through the experiences, he was still in awe of all that had happened in his life.

* * * *

Early the next morning, the two couples were ready to go shopping. Jeff knew the girls were more excited about going to the jewelry store than he and Karl were. Even though he knew he could afford any ring Marie picked out, he still worried about how extravagant she might be.

By noon, they had been to two jewelry stores with no luck in locating the perfect ring. He was about to give up when Jenny suggested they visit a small shop she'd been told about. Jeff was surprised to see an older man standing behind the counter and his Native American heritage was evident in his features.

"Marie, I'm pleased to have you come to my shop. What can I help you find?"

Jeff saw Marie's face brighten. "I'd forgotten you had this shop, Mr. Red Cloud. This is my fiancé Jeff Cooper. Mr. Red Cloud is the grandfather of my best friend Susan. Of course you haven't met her because she's working with her husband in one of the outlying villages in Alaska."

Jeff shook the older man's hand, wondering what he was doing living in a big city like Helena rather than on the reservation.

This man was drawn to this city in his old age because of his jewelry design. Although he lived his life on the reservation, he has made the people of this city aware of the artistic design of our people.

Jeff silently acknowledged the words of his Spirit Guide. As soon as he did, the old man brought out a tray of rings that caused Marie to gasp in delight.

"Aren't these gorgeous?" she asked as she picked up an engagement ring with a blue diamond set in a Black Hills gold setting. Although the diamond was unpretentious, the setting looked like an eagle holding the gem in its beak. The matching wedding band was beautifully etched to resemble the feathers of an eagle's wing.

"You have made a good choice, Marie. I just finished this set, as well as the others on this tray, but this one was my favorite. There is a matching band for the man you are marrying. I did not know why I created this design, but now I know it was meant for you. It came to me in a dream."

Jeff took the ring from Marie and knew, immediately, it didn't matter how much he had to pay for it because it was exactly what both he and Marie wanted. Dropping to one knee, he took Marie's left hand in his. "Marie Turtle, will you do me the honor of becoming my wife?"

Tears sparkled in Marie's eyes as he slipped the ring on the third finger of her left hand. "I've said yes to you once this week, and I say yes now, but can you afford this? It's the most beautiful ring I've ever seen and the fit is perfect, but we haven't even asked about the price. I don't know much about diamonds, but I have read that the blue diamond is very rare."

"The price doesn't matter. I have a feeling this ring was made especially for you. If not knowingly, then through the dream planted in Mr. Red Cloud's mind by our Spirit Guide."

While Marie and Jennie oohed and awed over the beauty of the diamond, Jeff talked with Mr. Red Cloud over the cost of the unique wedding set. When the old man named his price, Jeff was shocked. "You deserve much more than that for your work to say nothing of the stone."

Mr. Red Cloud smiled. "This ring was a labor of love. As for the stone, it is one I acquired when I was a young man and just beginning my business. I've always known of its worth as well as its beauty. In all the years I've had it in my possession I have never felt compelled to set it into a piece of jewelry. In my dream I was told I would be making it for a very powerful shaman to give to the woman he loved. I have long known of Marie's calling, and have heard about you from my son. He says you have been sent to take the place of my old friend, Alan. I am sorry to hear his life is coming to an end. As young men, we both dreamed great dreams. His was to be a shaman for our people while mine was to be a great craftsman. We have both lived our lives as we said we would, and now we are looking forward to walking with the ancestors. You and Marie are destined to carry on for Alan, while my oldest grandson has been training with me to take over my shop. Now that the ring is with its rightful owner I can turn over the shop to my grandson, and return to the reservation to spend whatever days I have left with my old friend."

Jeff took a deep breath. In his mind, he could see Alan and his friend enjoying each other as much in the next life as they had in this one.

With the rings paid for and the wedding set securely in his possession, Jeff thanked Mr. Red Cloud and turned to join his friends. Before they left the shop, Marie hugged the old man and told him she would tell her grandfather of how he would soon be reunited with his old friend.

Outside of the shop, Marie held up the ring to the spring sunlight, and Jeff noticed the way it sparkled even more in the natural light than it had in the artificial light of the shop.

"The old man was right," Karl said. "This ring was meant to grace your finger, Marie." Turning to Jeff he continued, "What happened in there? Did you have a vision? I felt as though we lost you just like we did the first time you saw the picture at the restaurant."

"You probably wouldn't believe me if I told you."

Karl gave a nervous laugh. "I'm beyond being skeptical where you're concerned, so you might as well tell us what went on in there."

"I heard the voice of my Spirit Guide telling me why Mr. Red Cloud was in Helena, rather than on the reservation of his birth."

Marie nodded her head. "I've always known about why he left the reservation, but I'd forgotten about the shop he has here. Growing up, he and Grandfather were best friends in the same way as Susan and I have been all our lives. The grandson he talked about leaving his shop to is Susan's older brother, Jon. I heard he'd moved to Helena right after high school. I just figured he was like so many other young men, and was looking for excitement in the big city. I didn't realize he was following in his grandfather's footsteps."

Jeff knew his friends had a hard time understanding and accepting the talk about Spirit Guides and the fulfillment of prophesies. Rather than continue the conversation, he decided it was time to suggest getting some lunch.

"This is your town, Karl. Where do you suggest we go for some lunch?"

Karl thought for a moment before guiding them to a small restaurant on one of the side streets away from the hustle bustle of the city. "This time our meal is my treat. After the bundle I'm sure you dropped on those rings, I'm afraid you'll be living on bread and water for some time to come."

"I'm not going to turn down your offer, buddy. Of course, I didn't spend as much as I thought I was going to on the rings."

"What do you mean?" Marie asked.

"When I went to pay Mr. Red Cloud for the rings, I couldn't believe the price he quoted me. I tried to pay him more, but he wouldn't hear of it. He believes he was guided by our Spirit Guide to make these rings for you and me. A year ago I wouldn't have believed any of this, but so much has happened I don't doubt anything anymore."

160

Chapter Twenty-Two

By Monday morning, everyone on the reservation was talking about Jeff and Marie's engagement as well as the wedding that was planned for the end of May. The other topic of conversation was word that William Red Cloud was returning to the reservation.

"I can't believe I will be reunited with my lifelong friend," Alan said at supper on Monday evening. "I was afraid we wouldn't be together again until we were both walking with the ancestors. I feel the way I did when we were kids. I'd wake up every morning excited about what Will and I would be doing together that day. Now in just over a week, we will be having new adventures to anticipate."

Jeff and Marie exchanged knowing glances. Because of the advanced age of the two old friends, it was a given, their new adventures would be in stories told from the comfort of their recliners.

"I'm looking forward to seeing Mr. Red Cloud again as well," Jeff admitted. "He has a wonderful talent, and I'm sure he will become the perfect role model for the students at the high school. I'm hoping to find more artisans like him for the career fair I'm planning for next fall at the school."

"Do you have any other people in mind?" Donna asked.

"As a matter of fact I do. I'm planning on having your daughter and son-in-law talk about opening their diner, Suzie Hawk for her regalia designs and Miranda Rabbit for her dream catchers and beadwork. With Mr. Red Cloud, I think the kids will get some great ideas of how they can break the stereotype of the lazy Indians who are hooked on booze and drugs."

Jeff's idea met with approval from everyone at the table. Everyone had ideas of other people from the reservation who might be interested in

161

participating and helping to shape the futures of the young people at the high school.

Their discussion was interrupted by a knock at the front door. Marie motioned for her mother to remain seated at the table and got up to answer the door.

"Mr. Red Cloud," she exclaimed, alerting everyone to the identity of their visitor.

"Here I'm Will, just like I've always been, my dear. I was hoping I was in time for one of your mother's delicious suppers. I'm certain the cupboards at my house are bare and will be until I go shopping tomorrow."

Donna was on her feet immediately. "There's always plenty to eat, as you should know. It won't take me but a minute to set another place at the table."

Alan moved over his plate while Jeff brought another chair to the table. Once Will was seated next to his childhood friend, Alan held out his hands to give another prayer over the food that was still in bowls on the table.

"Dear God and Great Spirit, bring blessings to this table and all who are joined here. My life has come full circle, and you have reunited me with the man I consider my best friend. Bless the food we are about to consume as well as those who will bring our people into the next phase of the life you have laid out for us."

Jeff considered the prayer and hoped he was worthy of the mission set before him. Considering he had no idea of his life calling just one year ago, he now saw it as something predestined by the Great Spirit as well as his Spirit Guide.

Throughout the meal, the two old friends reminisced, and Jeff enjoyed hearing stories of when the men were young boys growing up on the reservation.

After supper, everyone adjourned to the living room for coffee and dessert. Once they were seated, Will turned the conversation to Jeff and Marie and the future they were looking forward to.

"The 'blue' looks beautiful on your hand Marie," Will commented.

Jeff listened while everyone added their own comments about the engagement ring on the third finger of her left hand.

"I've done some research on blue diamonds," he finally said. "They are very rare. I know I didn't pay you nearly enough for the wedding set."

Will smiled and then laughed heartily. "Many years ago when I first started my business in Helena, I received the 'blue' in a shipment of diamonds. As soon as I saw it, I realized it was sent in error. I immediately contacted my supplier to tell him what I'd found and make arrangements to return it. When I finally talked to him on the phone, he laughed and told me he'd received the 'blue' in a special shipment, and like me called his supplier to report it. When he did, the man told him if the 'blue' had been perfect, it would have been worth much more than any other diamond. Unfortunately, the stone had a small flaw so they passed it on, hoping it would be sent to a jeweler who would have someone special in mind to wear it proudly. Because of its color and the flaw, my supplier sent it on to me. It has sat in my safe for over thirty years until I heard of the coming of Blue Eagle Feather. The Great Spirit came to me in a dream, and told me this special young man would be coming to my shop looking for a special ring for a special woman. That said, I designed the ring and kept it until the day you and Marie came into my shop."

"But—but, how did you know we would come to you?" Marie stammered. "We went to two other shops before we came to yours."

"I had faith in what the Great Spirit told me in my dream. As you now know, you found nothing in those other shops because this ring was the one that was destined to grace your hand. Considering you are both shaman, I'm sure you can understand the symbolism of the 'blue' and how it relates to our people."

"It is perfect for the woman I plan to make my wife," Jeff said with pride. "I knew as soon as I slipped it on her finger, and found it to be a perfect fit, that it was made especially for us. I can't begin to thank you for your hard work, and the beauty of the setting. Even though I know I didn't pay nearly enough for it, I thank you for such a perfect gift to seal our new lives together."

As the evening drew to a close, Jeff realized it was time to go home and prepare his lessons for the next day. "Are you ready to go home, Alan?" he asked, as he got to his feet.

"For tonight, I will be staying at Will's home. We have much to catch up on. I'm sure you understand."

Jeff nodded. He thought of his grandfather and the many nights he suggested Jeff stay with friends, so he and the other elders could spend the evening talking over things concerning the reservation as well as memories of their youth.

* * * *

The house was dark when Jeff arrived, but he sensed someone or something was waiting for him in the darkness. After parking his vehicle in the garage, he closed the garage door and made his way to the front door of the house.

"Mr. Cooper," Philip Wolf said as he stepped out from the shadows cast by the house. "I was wondering if I could talk to you."

After the initial shock of having someone waiting for him, Jeff invited Philip into the house. "Is there a problem, Philip?"

"Yes, sir. I just found out my girlfriend, Janet Elkhorn, is pregnant. Her parents want her to either have an abortion or give the baby up for adoption. I don't know what to do. I don't want my baby being given to strangers or worse yet, be killed. I know there's no one on the reservation who could take the baby and give it a good home. Everyone is struggling, just like my parents are. I suggested Janet and I get married, but her parents said they won't sign for her and mine said the same thing. They said we both need to get our educations and we're too young to be committed to one another in that way. What are we going to do, Mr. Cooper?"

Philip's confession hit Jeff like a slap in the face. "There will be no decision made tonight. Let me pray on it and arrange for a meeting with everyone over the weekend. For now, you need to get your rest. I'm sure you and Janet haven't had much sleep knowing what has happened. Do you know when the baby is due?"

"You're right about that. Janet and I have known for about a month, and just got up the courage to talk to our folks. The baby is due in September."

Jeff did a little mental math, and realized if the child was due in September it might already be too late for an abortion. Knowing nothing could be done tonight, Jeff decided to drive Philip home and take the time to talk to his parents.

Lights burned brightly in the windows of the Wolf home. Jeff took a deep breath knowing how worried Mr. and Mrs. Wolf must be. His knock was answered immediately. Mrs. Wolf's face was tear streaked when she opened the door.

"Oh, Philip, we were so worried. Where have you been?" As soon as the question was asked, she looked past Philip to see Jeff standing on her doorstep. "Mr. Cooper? Has Philip been with you? We've been sick with worry."

"May I come in, Mrs. Wolf?"

She stepped aside to give him access to the kitchen. "Philip was waiting for me when I got home from dinner. He told me of the situation he and Janet are in. Have you and the Elkhorn's come to any decision?"

Mrs. Wolf shook her head. "They're much too young to be getting married. They both have their educations to think about. I think the only thing we can do is look into ending the pregnancy."

"I think this needs a little more thought. If my calculations are correct, it's already too late for an abortion. Philip told me the baby is due in September. After the first trimester, abortion is not recommended. I want to do some praying, and some research and meet with both families on Saturday morning. Are you willing to meet with me?"

Mr. Wolf had a serious expression on his face. "Do you think you can come up with a solution to this?"

"It's possible, but I as I said, I have to do some research before I say something I shouldn't. I'll contact the Elkhorn's and see all of you on Saturday morning at my place, shall we say about nine?"

Once the Wolf's agreed, Mrs. Wolf placed a call to the Elkhorn home, and confirmed they would also be able to be at the meeting.

On the way home, Jeff called Marie. He prayed she'd still be up.

"Is something wrong?" she said as soon as she answered his call.

"You might say that. Have you gone to bed yet?"

"Are you kidding? I just finished grading papers. Why? What's up?"

"Is there any chance you can meet me at the house? This isn't something we should go into over the phone."

After making the short drive home, Jeff contemplated what he wanted to say to Marie while he waited for her to arrive.

"So what's so urgent it couldn't wait until tomorrow?" Marie said once she accepted a cup of coffee from Jeff.

"What would you think about becoming an instant family?"

Her expression was one of shock. "Are you telling me you just found out you got some girl in trouble back in Wisconsin?"

"Hardly. When I got home, Philip Wolf was waiting for me. It seems he and Janet Elkhorn are the ones in trouble. Their folks are talking abortion, but I'm afraid it's too late for that. They're also talking about putting the baby up for adoption, but do you know of anyone on the reservation who could take on a newborn in addition to their existing family? That said, maybe we could adopt the child."

Marie smiled, a look of relief on her face. "As a matter of fact I do. I told you about Will's granddaughter, Susan. She and her husband are returning to the reservation since their assignment in Alaska is over and are being reassigned here. The problem is, she can't have kids. I talked to her after everyone left Mom's tonight. She's thrilled about coming home, but is devastated by the news of not being able to have a child. We could call them now. With the time difference, it won't be too late up there. I'm sure they'd be thrilled to think there will be a chance to be parents after all."

Jeff waited while Marie placed the call to her friend. Once Susan answered, Marie put the phone on speaker so Jeff could hear their conversation.

"I'm surprised to hear from you again," Susan answered.

"I'm just as surprised to be calling you. I know you're coming for the wedding, but when will you be here permanently?"

"I'll be flying back right after the wedding to pack everything up so we can be there permanently by the 4th of July. Why?"

"It seems there are two of our students who are in trouble. Both sets of parents are all for terminating the pregnancy, but it's too late for that. What would you think about adopting the baby?"

"You're kidding, right? We'd be thrilled. We looked into adoption up here, but it would mean staying in Alaska, and we aren't prepared to do that. We're needed in Montana, and we wouldn't have any jobs if we stayed. Do you think they would be willing to let us adopt the baby?"

"I'm sure they would," Jeff assured her. "If you weren't willing to think about this I was going to ask Marie if we could adopt the child."

"Don't even think about it. We want a child so badly, and can't have one of our own. If we could adopt it, the birth parents could be in its life. My husband, Jim, is listening in on this conversation, and right now he's grinning like a Cheshire cat. I can hardly wait to get there for the wedding and meet the parents."

"Will you be available on Saturday? I'm having a meeting with both families, and would like to have you on the line at the same time."

It was Jim who answered with an enthusiastic yes.

Tears rolled down Marie's cheeks when they ended the call. "It's as if the Great Spirit is orchestrating this. If I hadn't called Susan tonight to make arrangements for the wedding, I wouldn't have known she just learned about not being able to have children. It's not like I wouldn't have wanted to adopt Philip and Janet's baby, but we have plenty of time to have children of our own. For Susan and Jim, it's the ideal solution to their problems. We would have been selfish to adopt the child when there were people who wanted a baby, but couldn't have one."

"I agree with you. By giving the child a loving home, I know we will make a difference in not only Susan and Jim's lives, but also in those of Phil and Janet as well as their extended families. I hope your friends will allow the birth parents to watch their child grow into a responsible adult."

Chapter Twenty-Three

On Saturday morning, everyone arrived at the house Jeff shared with Alan. Jeff felt it was best to be on neutral ground since both sets of parents had different ideas about the fate of their expected grandchild.

Brian and Carol Wolf with Phil in tow arrived first, followed closely by Andrew and Mary Elkhorn along with Janet. The looks passing between the two sets of perspective grandparents showed the difference in opinion of both camps.

"I think Janet should have an abortion," Mary declared. "I'm too old to start all over again raising a newborn."

Carol fumed before she exploded. "Who said you'd have to raise the child? If push comes to shove, I would take the child before I'd let some butcher kill it. In that way, the children could continue their educations. I know Phil is planning to go to college in the fall, and from what I've heard Janet is hoping to do the same thing."

It was Jeff who stepped between the two hostile mothers. "I think Marie and I have a solution that will be acceptable to both families."

"I don't want to kill my baby, Mr. C.," Janet cried.

"Just calm down and listen to what we have to say," Marie said. "I'm sure you all know Susan Red Cloud." Everyone in the room nodded. "Well, she and her husband, Jim Little Horse have been working in Alaska, but their assignment is over. She will be coming here for my wedding and will be making arrangements for them to relocate permanently. Jim is finished with his time working in one of the outlying villages as a medic, and they're both anxious to come home. That said, Susan thought they would be starting a family once they were stable, but she recently found out they can't have children. I've talked to her, and she is thrilled over the possibility of adopting the child. It would be an open adoption, and the child would always know their birth parents who were unselfish enough to realize they were too young to raise a child, and continue their educations."

"How do you know they'll allow us to be involved in our kid's life?" Phil asked, concern showing in his eyes.

"While we're all here we're going to do a Skype call with Susan and Jim," Marie explained. "As soon as we have them on line, I'm sure they will be able to answer all your questions."

It didn't take long before the miles between Alaska and Montana melted away. Jim and Susan appeared on the screen.

"It's so good to see you Carol, you too Mary," Susan greeted them. "Marie has told me about your dilemma. I know it's hard to accept when it's your kids, but for us it's a Godsend. Jim and I want children, but it seems we can't have any of our own. We looked into adoption, but we wouldn't be allowed to return to the reservation if we adopted a child here in Alaska, and we do want to come home. We also looked into adopting a white child, but we knew that wouldn't be fair to either us or the child."

"Can we be involved in the baby's life?" Janet said, still sniffing back her tears.

"We wouldn't want it any other way," Jim assured her. "We are so thrilled to think we will be able to raise a child of our people. It's imperative to us the child will know it's real parents, and be proud of the unselfish decision they made to give it a good life. I will be working as a paramedic with the fire department. Susan will be able to be a stay at home mother until it's feasible for her to return to work as a nurse at the hospital."

"I want to reiterate what Jim said," Susan added. "I am so thrilled to think I'll be able to stay home with our child until it's time for him or her to go to school. I'm glad you rebelled against your parents on the subject of abortion. Every life is precious and especially so for those of us on the reservation."

"I think you should be thanking Mr. C. He was the one who came up with this solution," Phil said. "He knew we didn't want to abort our child. I think the Great Spirit knew it too, and didn't want us to destroy a precious life. I know we're too young to be good parents, but since you are willing to adopt him, I think it's the best solution for all us."

Jeff listened to the exchange between the teenagers who were too young to become parents, and the couple who so desperately wanted a baby but couldn't have one naturally. *I pray I've helped these young people make the right decision.*

It took only a moment for the voice of Jeff's Spirit Guide to sound within the confines of his mind. *This was the first test of your judgment, my son. I am proud of the way you have stood up to this challenge. The child Phil and Janet have made will grow to be a productive member of the community, secure in the love of not only its natural parents, but also that of the man and woman who will raise it. There will be more tests to come, but you will master them with the same ease as you have shown today.*

"Are you with us, Jeff?" Marie asked, bringing him out of his communication with the Spirit Guide.

"Yes, yes of course I am." He turned his attention to Phil and Janet. "I was just thinking about the ease we were able to solve this problem. I'm not saying this pregnancy will be easy for either of you, but you must know the two people who will be raising your child will love it, and allow you to play a part in its life."

Janet's tears flowed down her cheeks almost like a waterfall over the edge of the chasm. "I know you're right," she finally managed to say. "I know I want to go to college and I also know I can't care for my baby. I am so grateful to Susan and Jim for their offer. It won't be easy to give my child away, but I know it's for the best."

Jeff listened as Marie continued her conversation with Susan. He could see the relief mirrored in the eyes of both sets of parents. No matter what Carol said, he knew she wasn't thrilled about raising a grandchild when her own children were on the verge of becoming adults and leaving the home. As for Mary, even though she was the one in favor of the abortion, he knew she was relieved to know her grandchild would grow up in a loving home while her daughter continued her education.

* * * *

By Saturday evening, Jeff felt completely drained. As soon as everyone left his house after the Skype call, he'd made an excuse of wanting to be alone to go out to the teepee to pray to the Great Spirit about everything the morning had brought about.

It came as no surprise, when he went into a trance and his spirit left his body, and became one with the eagle. In his transformed state, he saw the future, and was pleased with what he saw.

Phil and Janet's child would be a girl, but one with a great future. In time, she would become a doctor and return to the reservation to do great work.

As for her birth parents, they would marry and have other children, but they would first get their college degrees, and return to also do great work for the people. Phil would get a degree in business, and become one of the managers of the plant that would be reopening in the near future, while Janet would get her degree in education and teach in the elementary school.

What are the other challenges you will be setting before me? He asked the giant eagle who sat in front of him.

You will know them when they come. For now, be confident the decision you have made is the correct one. Do not dwell on what is coming, but be prepared for whatever the future brings your way.

Chapter Twenty-Four

Marie took over the planning of the wedding, while Jeff spent long hours with Alan learning everything he could from the old man before the Great Spirit took his spirit to walk with the ancestors. The thought of Alan's death saddened him, but his communications with his Spirit Guide told him everything happened for a reason, and did so when the time was right.

By the last day of school, there was no hiding of Janet's pregnancy, but word of the adoption of the child spread like wildfire through the community. Many people told him how pleased they were with the solution he and Marie had come up with.

"I had a call from my Aunt Kelly," Jeff said once they finished eating dinner. "She and Uncle Mike will be arriving with Uncle Paul the first of next week. Thank goodness I have room for them at the house along with Uncle David and Aunt Betty."

"I know Grandfather is thrilled with all the preparations. I do worry this will be too much for him. He has no intentions of returning home. He's very comfortable staying with my mother. I'm glad the wedding is so close because I think his days in this life are coming to an end. He hasn't even wanted to go to the teepee to meditate. Yesterday he told me he has spoken with his Spirit Guide and was told your time is coming as his is ending. I don't know how we'll go on without him in our lives."

Jeff took Marie into his arms and kissed her tenderly. "I, too, have been in contact with our Spirit Guide, and he tells me the same thing. Life is gift, and so is passing to walk with the ancestors. As a kid, I always heard how the Indians always knew when death was coming. I saw it for myself when I lost my grandfather last summer. It's the same with Alan. He's been very busy making peace with everything and everyone in his life. He is preparing for what is to come and is welcoming it."

Marie nodded even though her tears dampened his shirt.

* * * *

The following week, the wedding guests began arriving at the reservation. It amazed Jeff at how thrilled he was to see all of his aunts and uncles. The original animosity he'd experienced with his paternal grandfather had not carried over to his father's brother and sister. The way they interacted with his maternal aunt and uncle was as though they'd been the best of friends for their entire life.

Although Jim couldn't make it for the wedding, Susan arrived on Wednesday and was anxious to meet with Phil and Janet.

Finally on Friday, Karl and Jenny drove up from Helena. Of everyone who came for the wedding, Jeff was the most excited about reuniting with his best friend from college.

"Are you getting wedding jitters, old buddy?" Karl asked once they were alone for the first time.

"I haven't had time to think about it. There's been a lot going on here, and I haven't had much time to give the wedding any serious thought. I'm looking forward to making Marie mine, but there is so much more happening."

"What do you mean?"

Jeff proceeded to tell Karl about Phil and Janet's pregnancy and the adoption he and Marie helped to initiate, as well as the ending days of Alan's life. "Marie is so close to her grandfather, I'm afraid his death will hit her hard. I've been through it less than a year ago, and I know how she's feeling. I just hope it won't devastate her too badly."

"Marie is strong, and I'm sure she'll do better with it than you think. Now let's talk about important things, like the bachelor party."

Jeff laughed for the first time. "There's not enough time for a bachelor party, and you have to remember there's no hard liquor allowed on the reservation. You'll have to be content with the rehearsal dinner Marie's mother is making for us tonight."

They talked for several hours until it was time to leave for the rehearsal. The minister at the church told them he had no problem doing a joint service with a shaman. Although Jeff wanted Alan to do the ceremony, the old man insisted it was his job to give the bride away. The duties reserved for the shaman then fell to Jeff's Uncle David. Alan assured them he'd instructed David as to the traditional Blackfoot marriage ceremony.

With the instructions on what would happen the next day finished, the wedding party went to Donna's house for dinner. As usual, she prepared a feast fit for a king. It amazed Jeff to see how many helpings of Donna's special dishes Karl managed to consume.

"That was some of the best meat I've ever eaten," Karl complimented Donna once he finally pushed away from the table.

Everyone at the table began to smile broadly. "Donna does have a way with preparing Elk."

"Elk?" Karl echoed Jeff's word, a look of shock on his face.

"That's right, old buddy, elk. I've been telling you for years what you're missing by not eating wild game. Now you can see for yourself what I've been talking about."

"I agree with Karl," Jenny said. "This has been a very special dinner, and I wish I could learn how to make wild game taste this good. Of course, I'd need a mighty hunter to bring it home to me. Unfortunately, my mighty hunter is a doctor and killing just isn't in his vocabulary. I have heard there is a meat market in Helena where I can purchase any kind of wild game. I have hesitated on purchasing any of it for fear of ruining it."

"I tell you what," Marie chimed in. "The next time we're in Helena, I'll bring you some elk steaks, and show you how to fix them. Mom taught me and I'm sure I can teach you."

Jeff contemplated the conversation and marveled at how well his college friends and his new Native American family were meshing together.

* * * *

The time for the wedding was set for eleven o'clock on Saturday morning. Rather than staying at the house the night before, Jeff bid his houseguests good night and made his way to the teepee Alan insisted now belonged to him. For this night, he needed to connect with the Great

Spirit as well as his Spirit Guide. All he told his houseguests was that he needed some time alone. If any of them knew where he went, it wasn't because he told them of his plans.

He built a fire in the fire pit when the evening turned cold. As the smoke was drawn up through the top of the teepee, Jeff could feel his spirit preparing to leave his body, and become Blue Eagle Feather, the mystical bird who could fly to the heights of the heavens and confer with those who now guided his life.

Tomorrow you will begin to walk on a new path, my son, the giant bird he equated with his Spirit Guide told him. *Until this time, you have had to think of no one but yourself, but now you will have a wife to love and cherish. Eagle Woman is your equal in more ways than you know. Her mind is sharp giving her the ability to teach the young people at the high school. Like you, she will help these young men and women to have the knowledge to change the future that looms ahead of them.*

Were we right to promise Phil and Janet's child to Susan and Jim? Should we have raised it ourselves?

You ask me to predict the future, but I foresee you and Eagle Woman bringing several children into the world, and teaching them both the way of the modern world and that of the ancients. It is important for you to keep the past alive while preparing them for the future.

His body stirred, urging his spirit to return to the present. Reluctant to leave the freedom of flying without being encumbered by his body, his spirit returned and Jeff awoke. The fire had died down to a few glowing embers and shafts of the first morning light came through the smoke hole.

This is my wedding day, he thought as he stretched and got to his feet. Making certain the fire was completely out, he hurried to leave the tepee and return to the house to prepare for the ceremony that would make Marie his wife.

Karl was sitting on the front porch enjoying a cup of coffee when Jeff pulled into the driveway. "Everyone in there was getting worried about you when you didn't come home last night. Your Uncle David was trying to tell them you were all right, but the Illinois relatives were skeptical."

"I should have told them where I was going and why, but at the time

I didn't think about it. I needed some time to meditate before beginning my new life. How did you do without your wife by your side last night?"

"With me working such crazy hours, there are a lot of nights when I don't make it home to sleep with her. I can imagine the girls had fun giving Marie all kinds of tips on being married and were up until the wee hours of the morning. I remember Jenny telling me how they had a real hen party when we got married."

"Hen party? That's an interesting way to put it. My grandfather used to say listening to the women talking was like listening to chickens in the hen house. From now on, I'll never look at a group of women the same way."

Karl laughed at Jeff's statement before the two of them went into the house so Jeff could have some breakfast before getting ready for the ceremony.

Chapter Twenty-Five

Jeff was glad the weather held so the outside ceremony at the sacred teepees could be performed and enjoyed by not only the people of the village but also the out of town guests. Once he and Karl finished eating the breakfast his aunts Betty and Kelly prepared, they excused themselves to dress for the ceremony that would be taking place in a few hours.

Jeff knew the white doeskin tunic and leggings with their beautiful beadwork and embroidery were an exact match for the dress Marie would be wearing. Karl on the other hand wore a tunic and leggings of the more traditional tanned leather which would also match the dress worn by Susan. All in all, he realized this would be a wedding his Illinois family would talk about for years to come.

The ceremony began with the Christian ceremony, where Jeff and Marie pledged their lives to one another until 'death do us part'. Jeff stood next to Karl, and tried to get his nerves under control as Susan walked down the makeshift aisle. He held his breath when Marie came out of the grove of trees with Alan at her side.

Marie's face seemed to glow in anticipation of the vows they would soon be exchanging. With each step she took to stand at his side, Jeff felt his heart beat a little faster, and the smile on his face become broader. It took her only a minimum of steps to stand close enough for him to be able to reach out and touch her.

"Who gives this woman to this man in matrimony?" the minister asked.

"I stand in the place of her father who walks with the ancestors. As his representative, I and Marie's mother give my granddaughter to this man who is her equal in every way." With that said, Alan leaned over and kissed Marie's cheek before he clasped Jeff's wrist as a symbol of acceptance.

As many weddings as Jeff had attended over the years, he knew the vows by heart, but he knew if he would be asked to tell anyone what he'd said, he would be hard put to remember. Marie's beauty mesmerized him so much he seemed to be in a daze, until he heard the minister pronounce them man and wife.

"You may kiss your bride."

The statement brought Jeff back to the present, and he obliged by taking Marie in his arms and giving her their first loving kiss of their married lives. He only broke the kiss when he heard the snickers of their guests at his show of affection for his new wife.

Once the ceremony was finished, the minister stepped aside to allow David Red Fox to take his place to begin the Blackfoot ceremony. Jeff had questioned Alan's suggestion of David taking over this part of the wedding, but there had been enough discussions between the two men over the past few days that it was clear his uncle knew what he was doing.

"To begin with, I would like to thank everyone who has come to see these two young people join their lives together, not only physically, but also spiritually. We have all witnessed Jeff and Marie pledging themselves to one another. Now it is time to join Blue Eagle Feather and Eagle Woman together in a bond that cannot be broken. Since each of them are shaman in their own right, they could pledge their love and seal their union without my guidance, but I am honored to be officiating at this portion of their wedding ceremony."

Jeff smiled broadly at his uncle. For a moment, he saw not his uncle, but his grandfather standing before him smiling at him, acknowledging his acceptance of Jeff's choice of a life partner.

At the same moment, the call of an eagle rent the air. Looking heavenward, Jeff saw an eagle circling above his head, giving credence to the joining of these two young people who saw him as their Spirit Guide.

It was evident they were not the only ones who saw the eagle, as around them their guests all looked upwards to the heavens. The white guests gasped at the beauty of the bird who gave his blessing to the union between Jeff and Marie.

"I have thought long and hard about what I would say on this special day," David said as he faced both of them. "I looked at many wedding ceremonies that have been performed by our people over the years. The one I decided on was the fire ceremony. For these two young people I think it is quite appropriate. Behind me, there are three piles of wood. The pile to the North represents Blue Eagle Feather's life before coming to this reservation, and falling in love with Eagle Woman." David paused for a moment, as one of the men from the village set the wood on the northernmost pile on fire. "The pile to the South represents Eagle Woman's life before she met Blue Eagle Feather." Again someone came forward to light the southernmost pile.

"By pledging yourselves to each other, the life you lived before this is in the past and your fires are joined. It is now time for you to pledge your lives one to another."

Blue Eagle Feather looked at the burning pile of wood that represented the life he'd lived as Jeff Cooper. With nothing rehearsed, he began, "I pledge to you my love for today, tomorrow, and forever. My past is what has shaped me as a man, and prepared me to become your husband and life mate. We have been joined in the eyes of the Christian God, and now I take you as my wife in the eyes of the Great Spirit and our Spirit Guide."

Eagle Woman smiled at his words, and looked longingly at the fire that represented her past life. "All my life I have been training for the day when a man would be sent to me by my Spirit Guide to become my life mate. I knew the minute I saw you my destiny was to be your wife. We have been joined in the eyes of the Christian God, and now I take you as my husband in the eyes of the Great Spirit and our Spirit Guide."

"You have pledged yourselves one to the other and now, is the time to join your fires as one."

Blue Eagle Feather stepped forward first and picked up a burning stick. At the same time, Eagle Woman took a burning stick from her fire and together they lit the center pile of wood. It was apparent the pile had been soaked with an accelerant because the flames came to life immediately. Once they did, the men who lit the original fires came forward to douse the individual fires leaving the communal fire to burn brightly in the sunshine of the May afternoon.

With the formalities over, Jeff was now free to claim Marie as his equal in the life that stretched before them.

* * * *

The community center had been decorated for the wedding reception. Tables were laden with enough food to feed everyone in attendance, and then some. The centerpiece of the buffet was the wedding cake Jeff's Aunt Kelly insisted on baking and decorating for the occasion.

In the corner opposite the buffet table, sat a table filled with wedding presents. Considering the financial situation of most of the people on the reservation, the outpouring of love from the people Jeff now called friends was humbling.

"Before we begin the festivities," Alan announced to everyone assembled. "I have an announcement to make. For many years I have been your shaman, but the days when I will walk with the ancestors is fast approaching. From this day forward, you will be blessed with two shamans like no others ever to serve our people before. My granddaughter, Eagle Woman, and her new husband, Blue Eagle Feather, will lead our people into a future that will be not only harmonious with the whites but also one in which our young people will become leaders and will prosper. I pray all of you will support, and love these new leaders as much as I do."

For a moment, the people assembled were so quiet Jeff could hear the individuals breathing. He looked into the eyes of his friends and neighbors, and saw not only confusion, but also tears at the thought of their beloved shaman's announcement he would soon be walking with the ancestors. With his prediction of the future, he'd given Jeff and Marie more power than either of them were prepared to handle.

"As many of you know, I am Jeff's Uncle David. There are many shaman, myself included, who are willing to give help to these young people, as they need it. I am certain neither of them will need our assistance, as over the past year I can see how my nephew has grown both in stature and in the powers endowed to him by his Spirit Guide. I know I am not the only one who saw the eagle giving his blessing to this union today. As we learned at the council of shaman held here in December, Blue Eagle Feather is the answer to the ancient prophesy given to the people by Soars With Eagles."

The room exploded with cheers and applause. After several minutes, Jeff held up his hand for silence and asked everyone to bow their heads as he blessed the food. As his first 'official' job as the spiritual leader for his people, Jeff worried he would not know the proper words, but as soon as he began, he realized he knew exactly what to say.

With the blessing over, students from the high school escorted the wedding party to their seats, and served them plates heaped with a sampling of all the food on the buffet table.

From the time he'd spent on the reservation, he could tell which woman made each dish they were sampling. It pleased him to see the way the people pulled together to give them a proper wedding reception.

"I'd like to propose a toast to the bride and groom," Jeff's Uncle Paul said as he got to his feet. "I have missed the first years of my nephew's life, and am pleased to be included on this special occasion. Even with the number of miles separating us, I pray we will become as close as we would have been if things were different. Today, I am proud of the man you call Blue Eagle Feather and wish him, and his bride, Eagle Woman, only the best in life." He held his glass of sparkling grape juice up, and everyone else in the room mimicked his actions.

"To Blue Eagle Feather and Eagle Woman," the wedding guests echoed.

"We have an announcement to make as well," Donna said once the crowd quieted down. "As a wedding present, my father-in-law, Alan Turtle, is giving these kids his house, free and clear. Since this is their wedding night, anyone who has been staying with Jeff will be staying with families from the village. It is only fitting the wedding couple spend their first night as husband and wife alone."

Jeff almost choked on his sparkling grape juice. He'd never expected Alan would give them the house he'd lived in since his arrival. There had been so much going on he hadn't given much thought as to where they would be living once they were married. Thoughts of where Alan would be living crossed his mind, but he'd put it to the back burner.

"It's—it's too much," he stammered. "We can't put you out of your home."

"You are doing no such thing," Alan replied. "You know I have been staying with Donna, and she has said I am welcome to stay until the end of my days. We complement each other well."

When Jeff looked into Marie's eyes, he saw tears glistening in them. "We thank you, Grandfather. I know how much you love the home you and Grandmother built. We will take good care of it, and you will be an honored guest whenever you want to visit us."

More toasts were given, and once the meal was finished and the cake was cut and distributed, the drummers and singers began to do some traditional music before the disk jockey played the popular music for the guests to dance.

By eight o'clock, the party was beginning to wind down. It came as a surprise when several men and women formed an escort to walk Jeff and Marie from the community building to the house that was now to be their own. At the front door, Jeff lifted Marie into his arms and carried her across the threshold into the house. Once he picked her up, the people who walked them home began to sing a traditional song that wished them well in their married life.

"We're alone at last," Marie whispered once they bid their friends good-bye and closed the door.

"Did you know about your grandfather's gift?"

"I had an idea of what he had in mind. It's the reason I haven't pressed you about where we would be living. For tonight we'll be sleeping in your room, but as soon as I can, I'll be redecorating the master bedroom for us."

Jeff kissed her hard, and then took her to the bedroom he'd been using to consummate their marriage. Tomorrow he would think more about their future. Everything had happened so fast, he'd had no time to make permanent plans. With the gift of a house to live in, he knew one more decision was taken off his shoulders.

Chapter Twenty-Six

Sunday morning Jeff and Marie were awakened by someone pounding on the door. Jeff cursed under his breath as he got out of bed, grabbed a robe and went to see who would be bothering them so early on the morning after his wedding night.

To his surprise, Jenny stood on his doorstep with tears running down her cheeks. "Karl sent me over to get you. It's Alan, he's in bad shape. He's asking for you and Marie. Karl and the doctor from the hospital are doing everything they can to keep him comfortable, but they both agree you should be there with him."

Jeff turned away from the door and almost bumped into Marie. "I've known this was coming. You've been so busy these last few weeks you haven't seen how he's been failing. I knew he was holding on until we were married, and he could give us this house and tell the people we would now be their spiritual guides."

As quickly as possible, they finished dressing and went over to Donna's where Alan lay on his deathbed. As soon as they entered the house, Jeff saw Donna sitting at the kitchen table holding a cup of coffee as though it was her lifeline. Betty and Kelly sat on either side of her trying to give her comfort.

Memories of his grandfather's death assaulted his mind along with those of the visitation and funeral for his Grandpa Cooper.

This is the way the Creator planned for our lives, he heard his grandfather speaking within the confines of his mind. *We are only on this earth for a limited time. Alan has known his time was limited, and he's been blessed to have you and Eagle Woman to take his place among the people. Your time has come as his is ending. The singers will be here soon to sing him across the barrier between the life he's lived, and his journey to walk with the ancestors. There are many of us here to welcome him, including his son who is anxious to be reunited with the father he left behind so many years ago.*

Jeff took a deep breath. His grandfather made sense. As he'd read in the Bible, for everything there was a season. Today was Alan's season to pass from life to death. It would do him no good to allow his emotions to cloud the beauty of his journey.

The downstairs bedroom smelled of the sage that was burning in a small bowl. Jeff knew he could thank Donna for lighting the sage to purify the room.

As soon as they entered the room, Alan held out his hands to them. "Last night I had a vision from the Great Spirit as well as my Spirit Guide. My time is coming, and they told me I would be allowed to say good-bye to both of you before I begin my walk with the ancestors."

"I don't know what I will do without you, Grandfather," Marie said, as she tried hard to hold back her tears.

"I will never be further away than your memories. I will always be there to guide you in everything you do. I have trained you well, and with Blue Eagle Feather, you will lead our people into the future. Your father is waiting for me and I am anxious to join him. My time on earth has come to an end, just as yours is beginning. Make me proud Eagle Woman."

Jeff watched as Alan took another deep breath and closed his eyes. Without thinking of what to do, Jeff started a chant to help Alan's spirit begin its final journey. Although he'd never done anything like this before, somehow he knew the tone of the chant as well as the words that were necessary to help Alan's spirit pass over.

It seemed as though he'd been chanting forever when Karl touched his arm. "It's over," Karl said. "I've never seen anyone pass so peacefully. I wish you could be with my patients when the end is near."

Jeff looked at his friend, unaware of what he was talking about. He'd done only what came naturally to him. He'd felt Alan's spirit leave his body, and in his mind's eye, saw him cross between the living and the dead. He'd even seen Alan being reunited with Marie's father. With one glance toward Marie, he knew she'd seen the same thing. Although they would miss Alan's physical presence, he realized the time was right for one generation to pass from life and another to take their place.

* * * *

The out of town relatives insisted on staying on at the reservation until after the funeral. The families who took them in never hesitated in telling them they were welcome to stay as long as they needed to.

It took only two days for the shaman who attended the conference in December to assemble in order to pay their last respects to the man many of them called a great shaman.

Although Jeff and Marie offered to open their home to the visitors, no one in the village would allow it. They contended as a newlywed couple, they needed their time alone.

By Wednesday, the village was filled to capacity with dignitaries who came to pay their respects to Alan, and take the burden of funeral preparations from Jeff and Marie. For this, they were both relieved, as they knew this would be one of the most difficult things either of them would have to do.

On the night before the funeral, Jeff and Marie went to the sacred teepees to pray and meditate. As much as Jeff wanted to be with Marie, he understood her need to be in her own teepee in order to meditate, and make contact with her Spirit Guide.

He'd just gotten his fire started when he felt his spirit ready itself to leave his body in order to make the contact he needed to with his Spirit Guide as well as the Great Spirit.

You have made the Spirit Guides proud, Blue Eagle Feather, the giant eagle who stood before him said. Even without knowing the words to the song of passing, you did what came naturally to you, and you eased the journey of Painted Turtle as he crossed from life to death. He now walks with the ancestors, and has begun on the path of his eternity.

I feel so inadequate. I wish Painted Turtle had been able to teach me more of what I need to know.

You know more than you think you do, my son. I will always be with you whenever you are in doubt. It will not always be necessary for you to shape shift in order to talk to me. Just call me with your mind, and I will answer. It will be the same with Painted Turtle as well as your grandfather. We are all here to help you on your journey, although you will not need as much help as you might think.

I feel so inadequate. All of the shamans I have ever known have trained their entire lives to walk the paths that have been laid out for them. I have not had the same training, and yet there are people here who look to me to be their spiritual guide. What if I do the wrong thing? What if my decisions are not the right ones for our people?

Do not dwell on the 'what ifs' in this world. When the time comes, you will make the right decisions because the Great Spirit and I will be with you to guide your thoughts.

As had happened before, a stirring in his body coaxed his spirit to return from its sojourn with his Spirit Guide. Reluctantly, he returned to the body waiting for him. Once he did, he felt another presence with him in the teepee.

Opening his eyes, he saw Marie standing next to him. "It's time for us to go back. I contacted with my Spirit Guide, and she gave me a vision of our future. Together we will shape the lives of our people and have a good life together."

* * * *

The morning of the funeral was dreary. It was as though the clouds were crying along with the people over the loss of Alan Painted Turtle. Because of the weather, the service was held in the community center and presided over by the shaman who just months earlier had met to discuss the future of the people.

Jeff sat beside Marie, knowing one day, he would be the one to perform the service of farewell for many residents of the village. More so now than in the past, he listened to the words the holy men were speaking.

"Oh, Great Spirit, accept the soul of our brother, Painted Turtle as he begins his journey to walk with the ancestors," Charles Hawk declared to begin the service. "During his time with us, he has been not only our friend but also the spiritual advisor for his people."

One after another, shaman as well as residents of the reservation, got to their feet to speak of the man all respected and who would be missed.

It surprised Jeff when Marie got to her feet. "My grandfather was a great man. As a child, I watched as he trained my father to follow in his footsteps. Unfortunately, the Great Spirit had other plans. When my father began his walk with the ancestors, my grandfather thought the last of his line was gone. That is when his Spirit Guide told him I would be the one to follow him. During my training, I questioned my ability, but my Spirit Guide assured me I would be provided a life mate who would complement the gifts my grandfather gave me. When Blue Eagle Feather came to us, Grandfather knew he would be the one to lead us forward. It was Blue Eagle Feather who eased Grandfather's passing from life to death. My husband and I will do our best to fill the void Grandfather has left in this village. We will make him proud of us."

Jeff wondered if he should say something, but realized Marie had said it all. In the silence that followed Marie's proclamation, the visiting shaman got to their feet in order to bring a conclusion to the Native American part of the service. It was then the Minister said words of prayer for Alan's soul.

Epilogue

With the funeral over, the village returned to normal. School that had been on recess since before Memorial Day weekend was in session. The extended Memorial Day holiday had put the kids a week behind in finishing their final exams, and ending their school year.

Now that life returned to normal, Jeff put Blue Eagle Feather to the back of his mind and concentrated on being Mr. Cooper, the teacher of history. As he waited for the first class of the morning to arrive, he took a deep breath.

Can I ever be Jeff Cooper again?

You never ceased being Jeff Cooper. The sound of his Spirit Guide's voice in his head came as a surprise. *You were born Jeff Cooper, and you were also born Blue Eagle Feather. The two are one, and now is the time when you must meld the two into one. We are all here to help you, but first you must help yourself.*

But how?

By doing what you do the best. By teaching the young people and helping them to reach for the stars and change their futures.

Jeff nodded his agreement. With the young people coming to him for guidance, and his Spirit Guide always ready to advise him on the way to go, he knew he could conquer his fears and lead his people into the future. No matter what he thought his shortcomings were, he now had the ability to do his best and become the man who would make his grandfather and everyone who came before him proud.

About the Author

Mild Mannered wife, mother, and grandmother by day, Sherry Derr-Wille spends her nights writing and writing and writing. Having been inspired by an English assignment in her sophomore year of high school, she had never quite finished the assignment. New stories pop into her head every day with never enough time to write them all.

A Wisconsin native, she grew up a country girl, but enjoys her 'city' home. She and her husband of over 50 years, Bob, live in a mid-sized town close to the Illinois border, where they are both enjoying their retirement. Deeming Bob 'A Saint' for putting up with her she has never regretted marrying her high school sweetheart just two days after graduation in 1964.

www.derr-wille.com

Read more by this author at
www.melange-books.com

Family Secrets
A Father's Love
Montana Rose
Hattie's Preacher, The Outlaw Series, Book 1
Outlaw's Son, The Outlaw Series, Book 2
Outlaw's Daughter, The Outlaw Series, Book 3